GUINEA PIG

PET SHOP Private eye

#3

The Ferret's a Foot

COLLEEN AF VENABLE

illustrated By

STEPHANIE Yue

z
z
z

GRAPHIC UNIVERSE™ · MINNEAPOLIS · NEW YORK

Story by Colleen AF Venable

Art by Stephanie Yue

Coloring by Hi-Fi Design

Lettering by Grace Lu and Zack Giallongo

Copyright © 2011 by Lerner Publishing Group, Inc.

Graphic Universe™ is a trademark of Lerner Publishing Group, Inc.

Graphic Universe™
A division of Lerner Publishing Group, Inc.
241 First Avenue North
Minneapolis, MN 55401 U.S.A.

Website address: www.lernerbooks.com

Library of Congress Cataloging-in-Publication Data

Venable, Colleen AF.
    The ferret's a foot / by Colleen AF Venable ; illustrated by Stephanie Yue.
        p.   cm. — (Guinea Pig, pet shop private eye ; #3)
    Summary: Enthusiastic sidekick Hamisher the hamster and reluctant detective
Sasspants the guinea pig investigate when their beloved home—Mr. Venezi's pet shop—
is vandalized.
    ISBN: 978–0–7613–5223–5 (lib. bdg. : alk. paper)
    1. Graphic novels. [1. Graphic novels. 2. Mystery and detective stories. 3. Pet
shops—Fiction. 4. Animals—Fiction. 5. Humorous stories.] I. Yue, Stephanie, ill. II. Title.
III. Title: Ferret is a foot. IV. Title: Ferret's afoot.
    PZ7.7.V46Fe 2011
    741.5'973—dc22   2010028272

Manufactured in the United States of America
5-44854-10878-10/13/2017

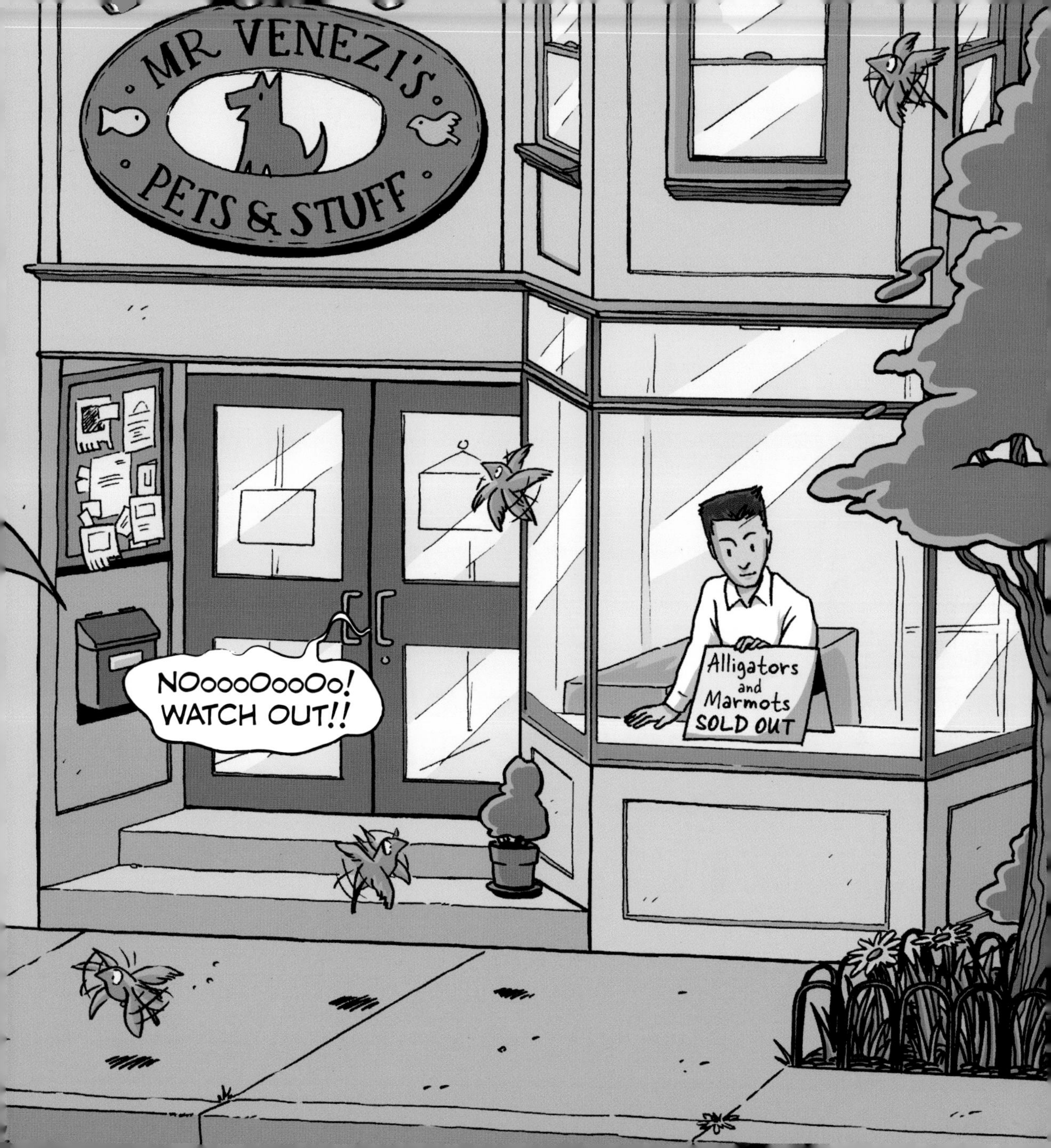
MR. VENEZI'S PETS & STUFF
NOooooOooOo! WATCH OUT!!
Alligators and Marmots SOLD OUT

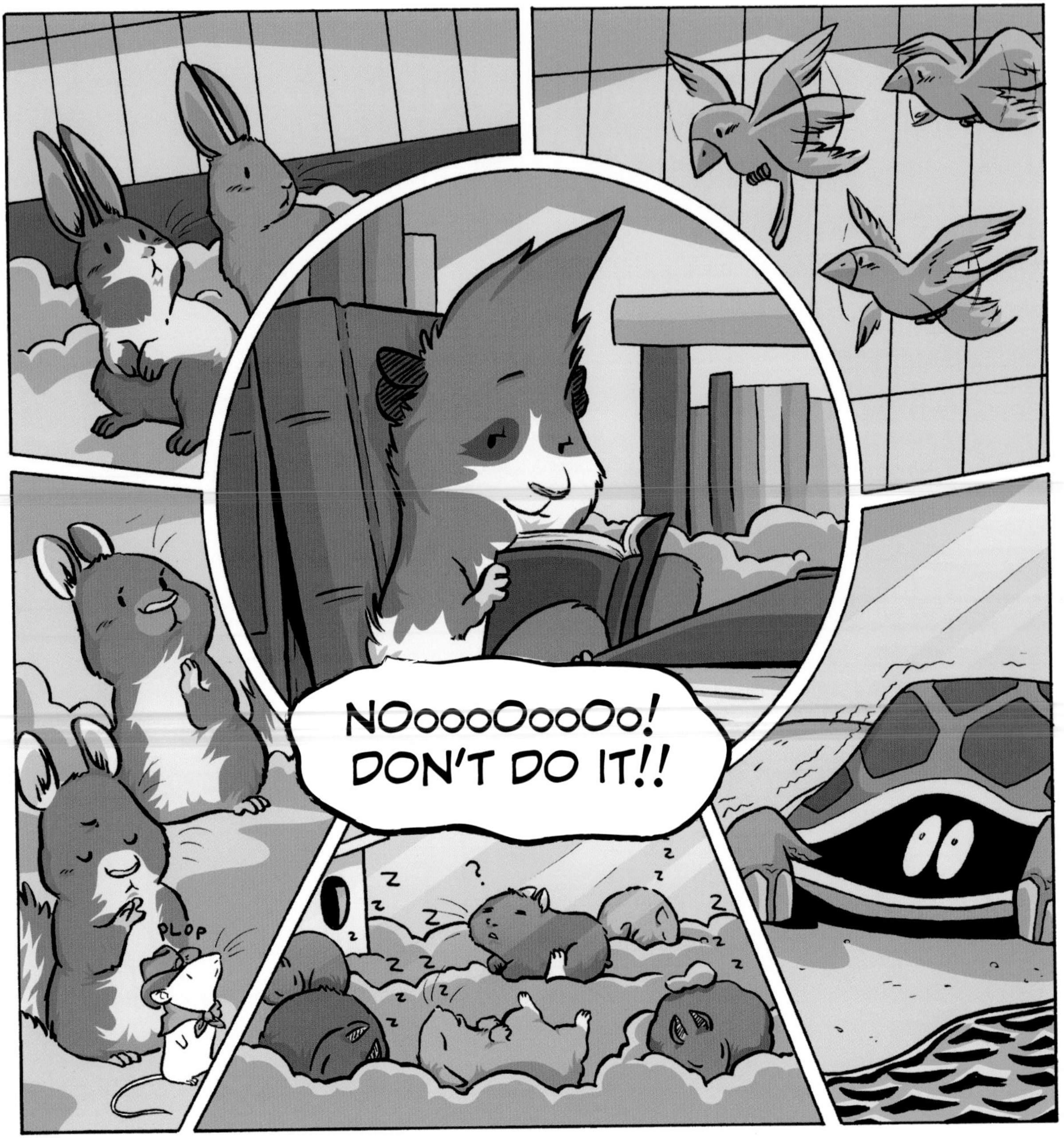
NOooooOoooOo! DON'T DO IT!!
PLOP

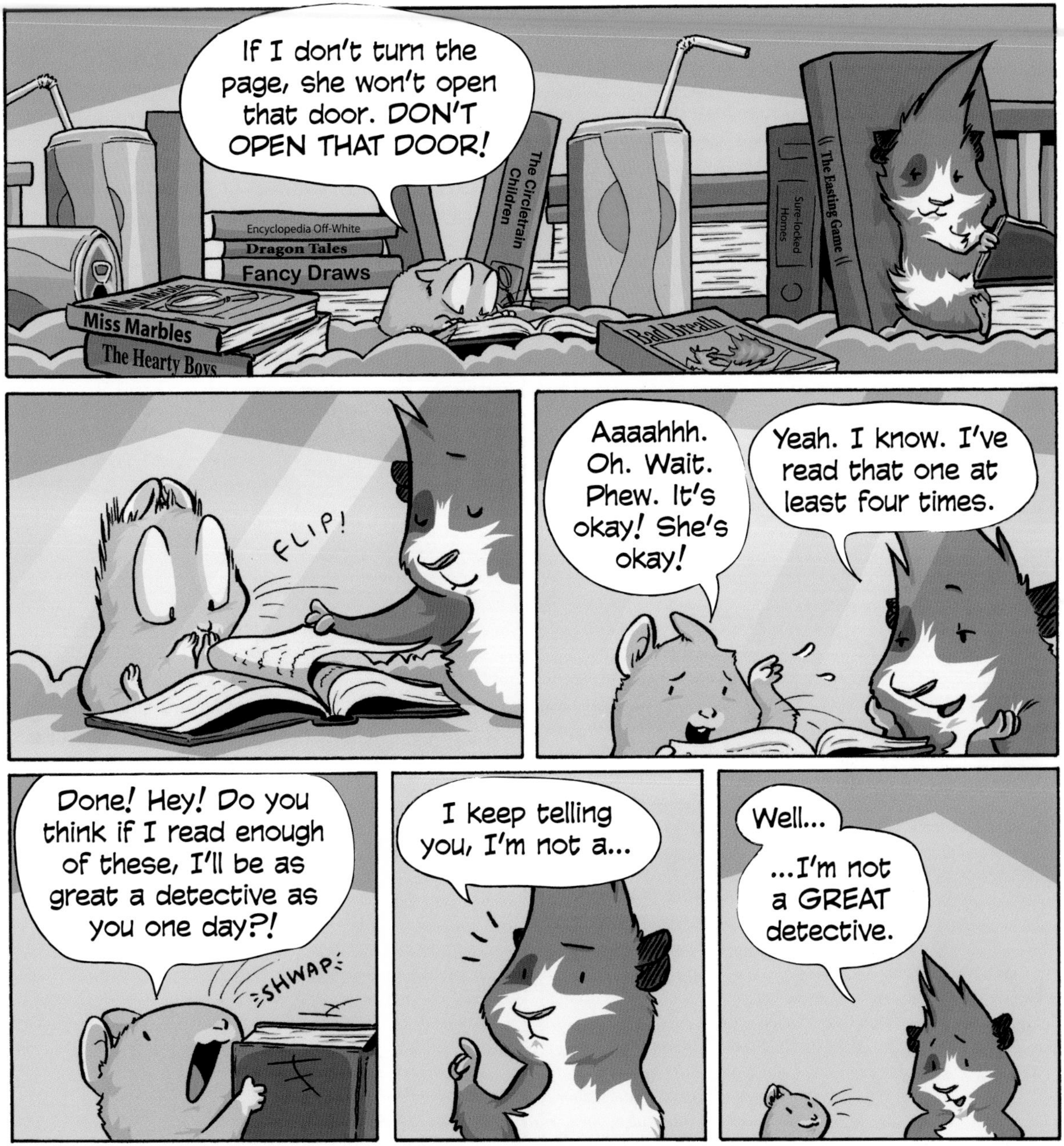
If I don't turn the page, she won't open that door. DON'T OPEN THAT DOOR!
Encyclopedia Off-White
Dragon Tales
Fancy Draws
Miss Marbles
The Hearty Boys
The Circletrain Children
Bad Breath
Sure-locked Homes
The Easting Game
FLIP!
Aaaahhh. Oh. Wait. Phew. It's okay! She's okay!
Yeah. I know. I've read that one at least four times.
Done! Hey! Do you think if I read enough of these, I'll be as great a detective as you one day?!
SHWAP
I keep telling you, I'm not a...
Well...
...I'm not a GREAT detective.

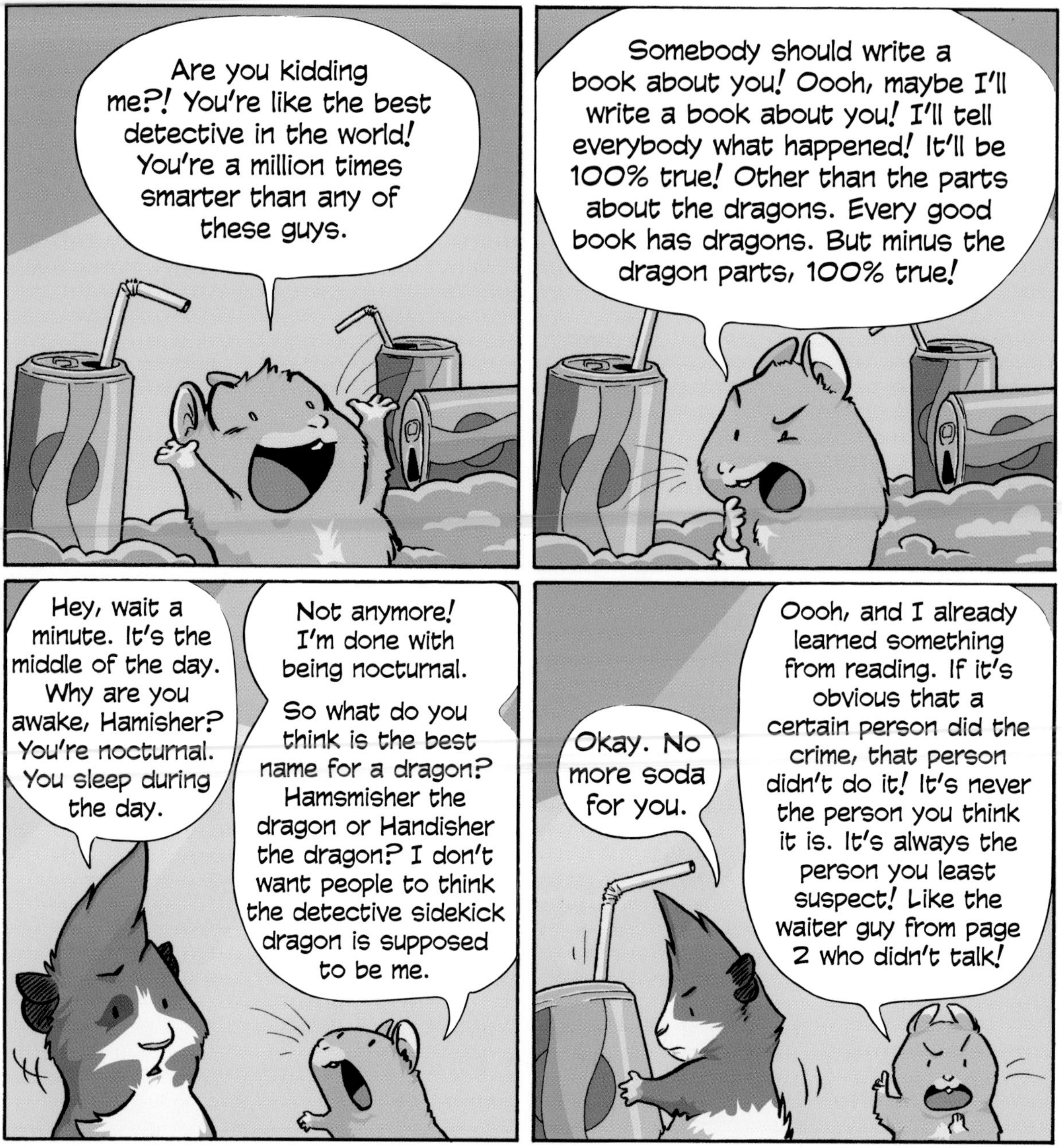
Are you kidding me?! You're like the best detective in the world! You're a million times smarter than any of these guys.
Somebody should write a book about you! Oooh, maybe I'll write a book about you! I'll tell everybody what happened! It'll be 100% true! Other than the parts about the dragons. Every good book has dragons. But minus the dragon parts, 100% true!
Hey, wait a minute. It's the middle of the day. Why are you awake, Hamisher? You're nocturnal. You sleep during the day.
Not anymore! I'm done with being nocturnal.
So what do you think is the best name for a dragon? Hamsmisher the dragon or Handisher the dragon? I don't want people to think the detective sidekick dragon is supposed to be me.
Okay. No more soda for you.
Oooh, and I already learned something from reading. If it's obvious that a certain person did the crime, that person didn't do it! It's never the person you think it is. It's always the person you least suspect! Like the waiter guy from page 2 who didn't talk!

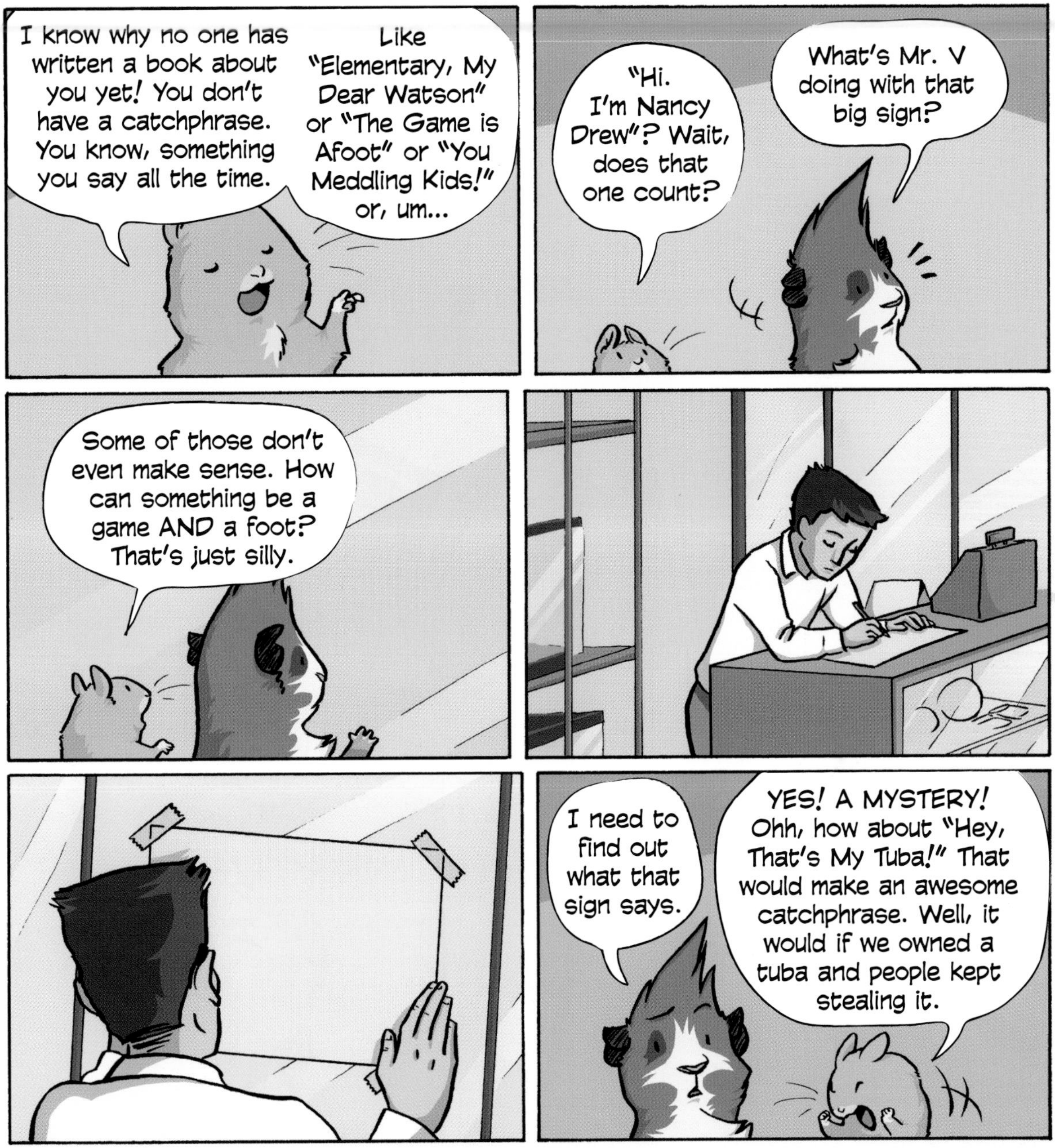
I know why no one has written a book about you yet! You don't have a catchphrase. You know, something you say all the time.
Like "Elementary, My Dear Watson" or "The Game is Afoot" or "You Meddling Kids!" or, um...
"Hi. I'm Nancy Drew"? Wait, does that one count?
What's Mr. V doing with that big sign?
Some of those don't even make sense. How can something be a game AND a foot? That's just silly.
I need to find out what that sign says.
YES! A MYSTERY! Ohh, how about "Hey, That's My Tuba!" That would make an awesome catchphrase. Well, it would if we owned a tuba and people kept stealing it.

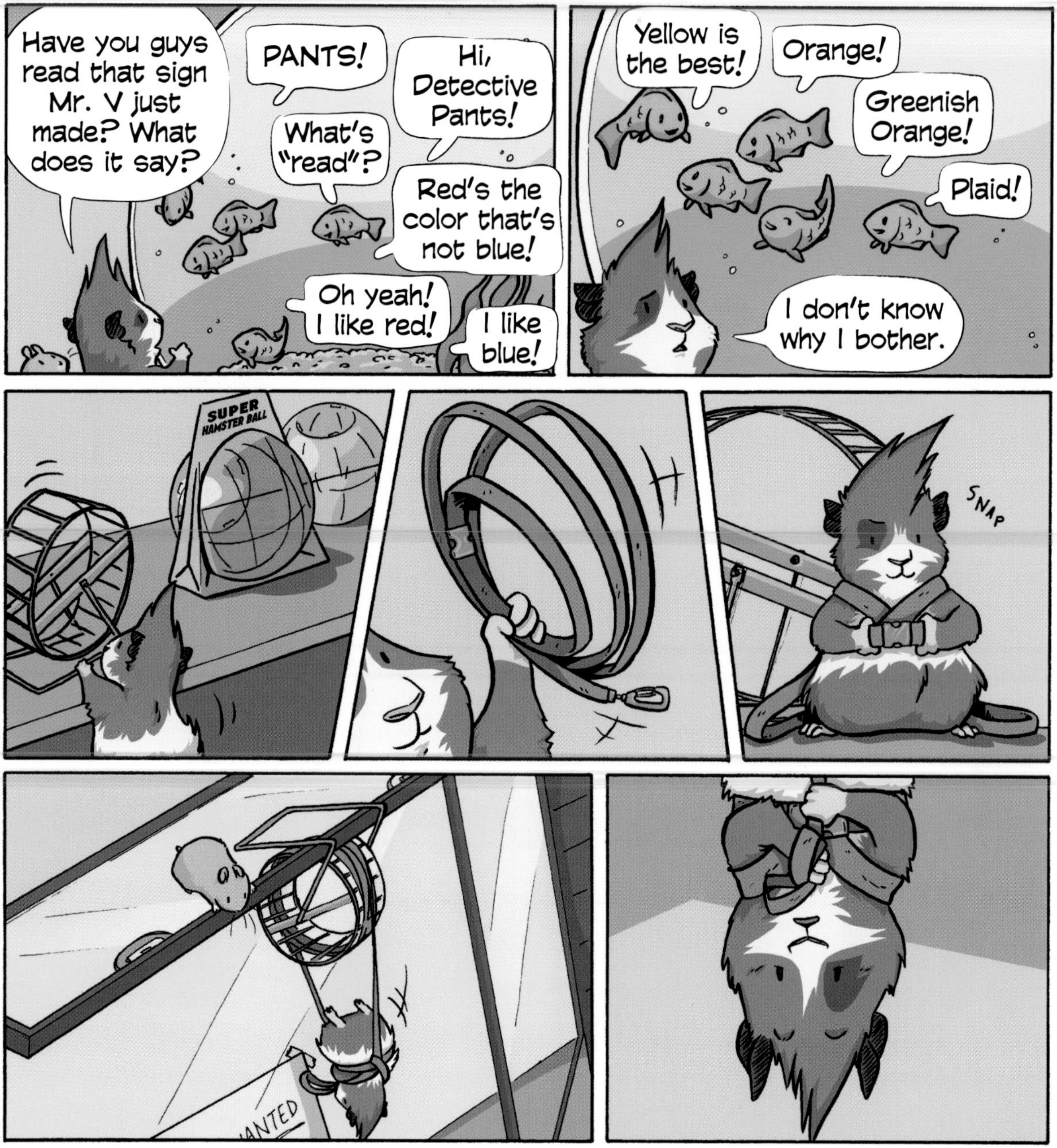
Have you guys read that sign Mr. V just made? What does it say?
PANTS!
Hi, Detective Pants!
What's "read"?
Red's the color that's not blue!
Oh yeah! I like red!
I like blue!
Yellow is the best!
Orange!
Greenish Orange!
Plaid!
I don't know why I bother.
SUPER HAMSTER BALL
SNAP
ANTED

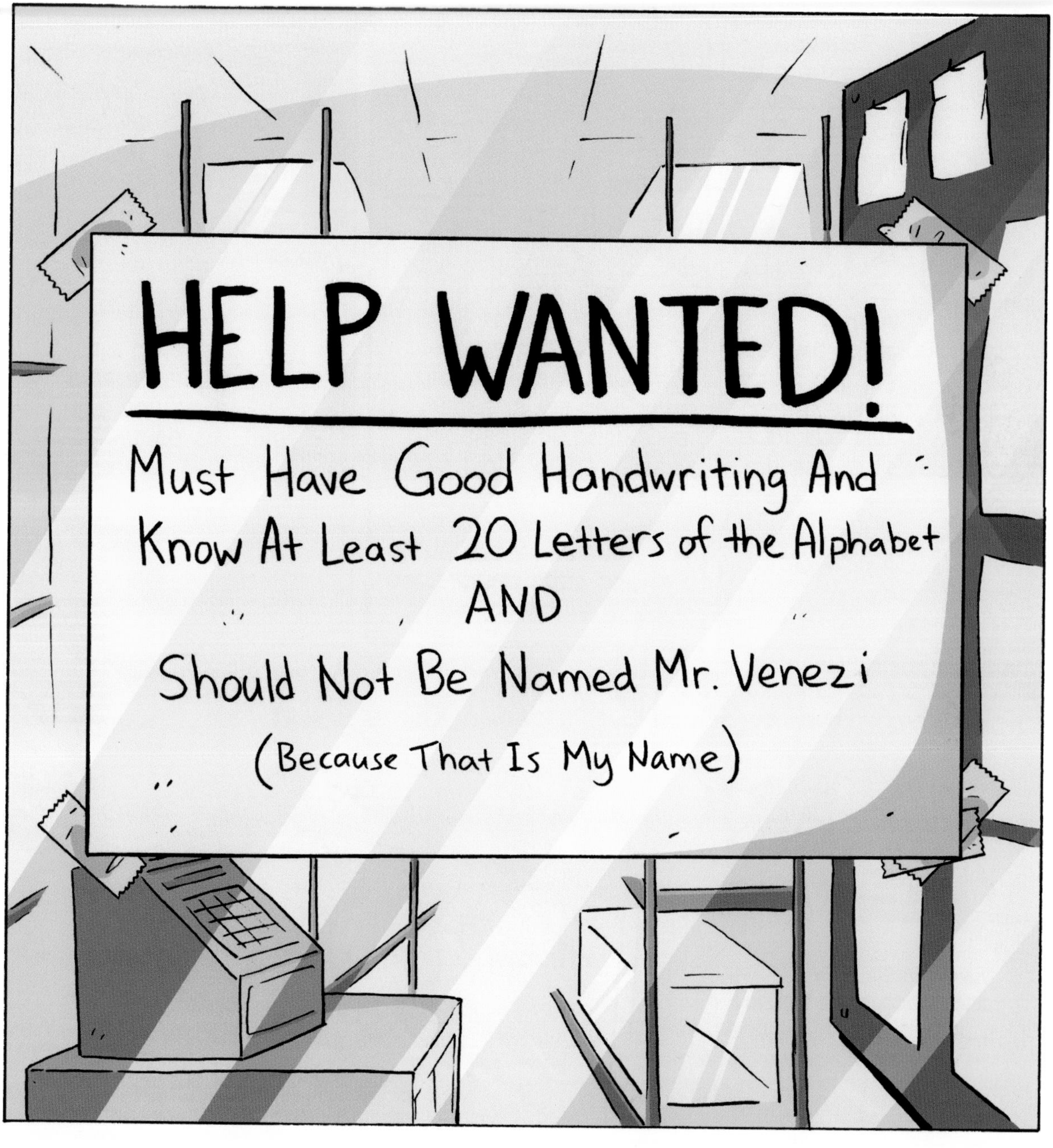
HELP WANTED!
Must Have Good Handwriting And Know At Least 20 Letters of the Alphabet
AND
Should Not Be Named Mr. Venezi
(Because That Is My Name)

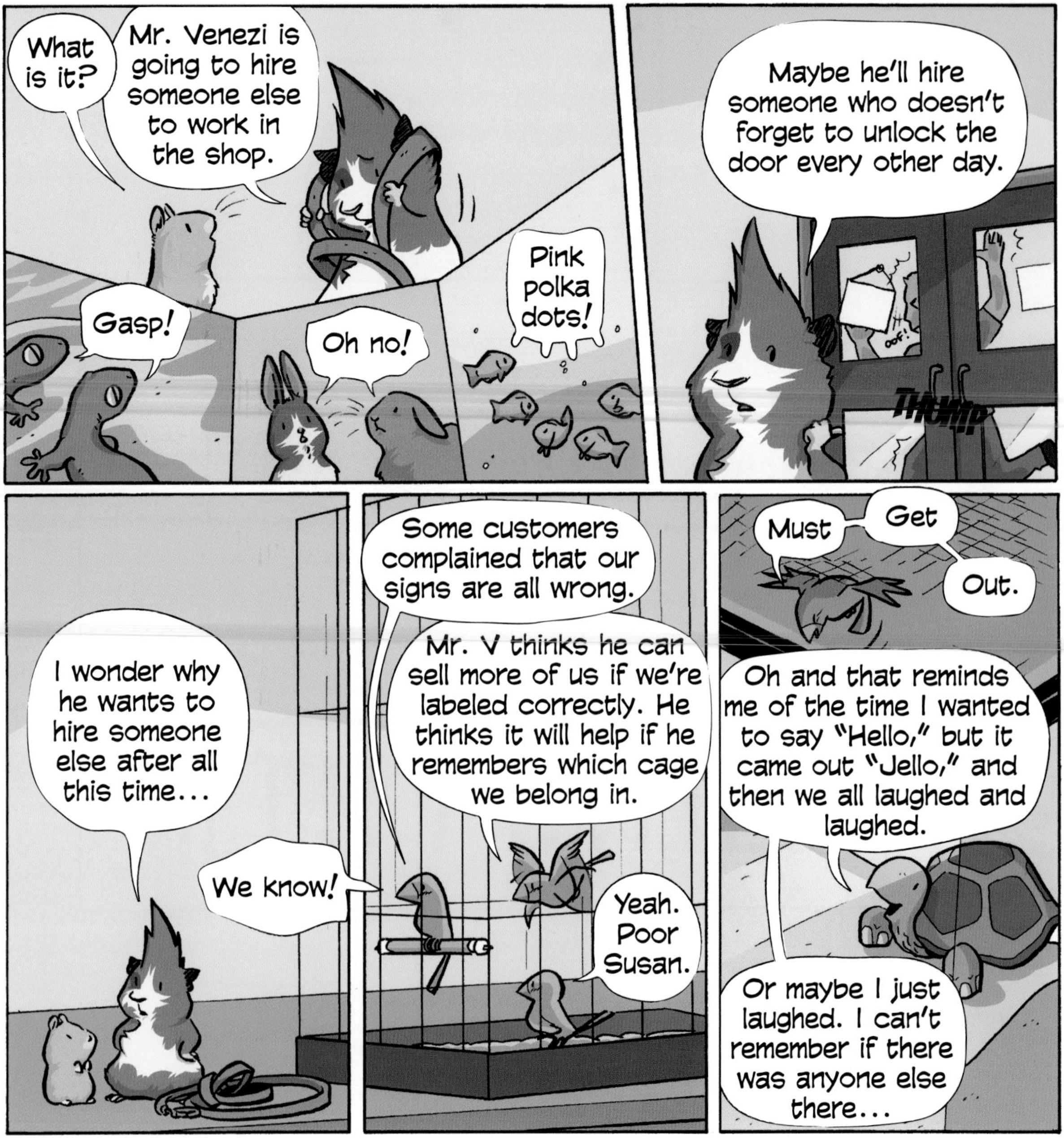
What is it?
Mr. Venezi is going to hire someone else to work in the shop.
Gasp!
Oh no!
Pink polka dots!
Maybe he'll hire someone who doesn't forget to unlock the door every other day.
OOF!
THUMP
I wonder why he wants to hire someone else after all this time...
We know!
Some customers complained that our signs are all wrong.
Mr. V thinks he can sell more of us if we're labeled correctly. He thinks it will help if he remembers which cage we belong in.
Yeah. Poor Susan.
Must
Get
Out.
Oh and that reminds me of the time I wanted to say "Hello," but it came out "Jello," and then we all laughed and laughed.
Or maybe I just laughed. I can't remember if there was anyone else there...

Hmmm. We can't risk Mr. V hiring someone.

BLINK
BLINK

That's it!

Huh?! What?! I'm awake!

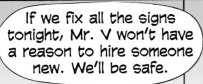

If we fix all the signs tonight, Mr. V won't have a reason to hire someone new. We'll be safe.

Brilliant!

Yes!

Wow. Herbert's STILL telling that story.

That was like the time someone called me Bert instead of Herbert. I laughed so hard my pants almost split. Why I was wearing pants, I'm not quite sure...

If I write on the signs and Hamisher draws a picture of the animal that should be in the cage, Mr. V won't get it wrong anymore.

How about it, Hamisher? Are you up for it?

I'm just going to take that as a yes.

11

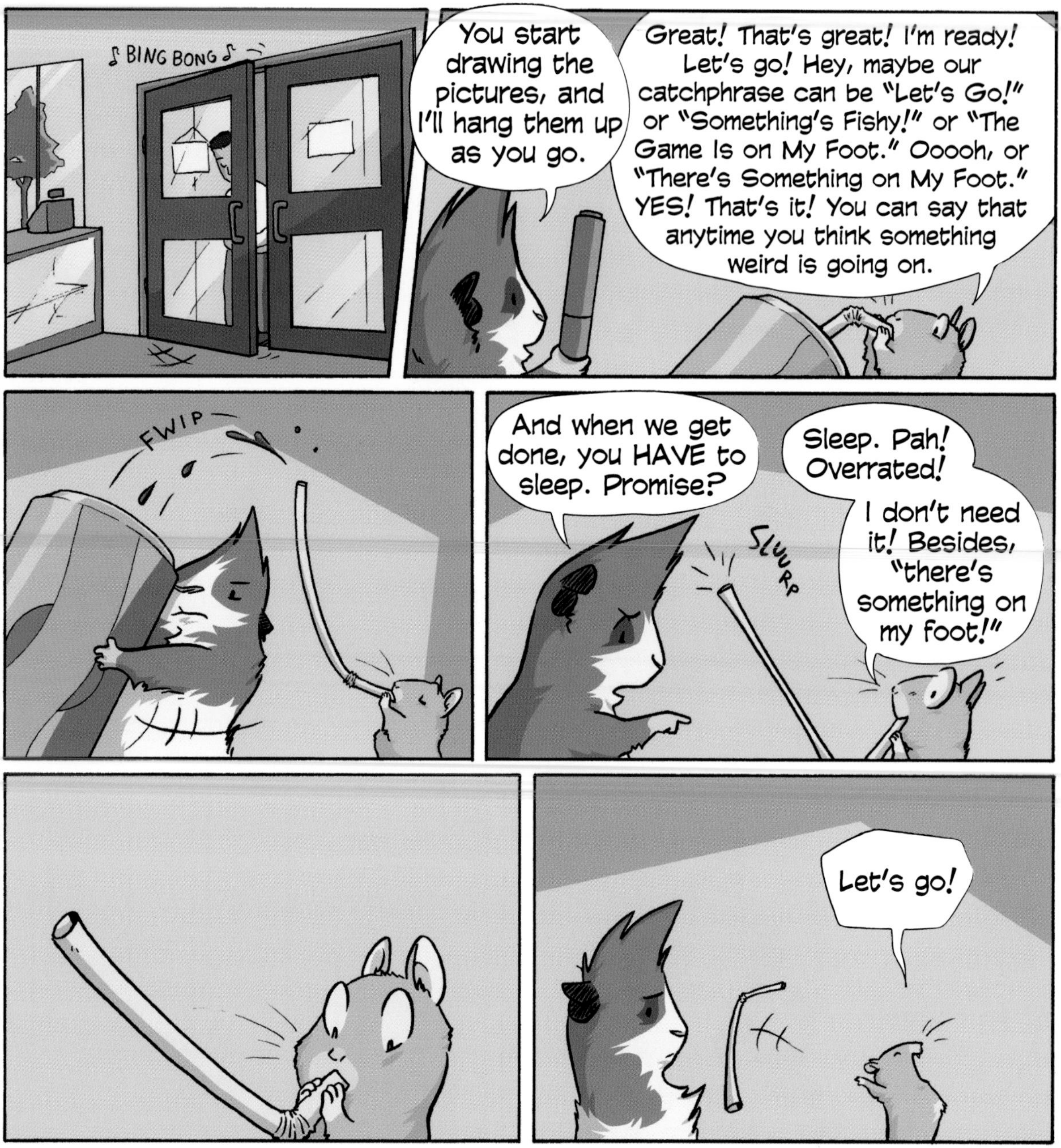
BING BONG
You start drawing the pictures, and I'll hang them up as you go.
Great! That's great! I'm ready! Let's go! Hey, maybe our catchphrase can be "Let's Go!" or "Something's Fishy!" or "The Game Is on My Foot." Ooooh, or "There's Something on My Foot." YES! That's it! You can say that anytime you think something weird is going on.
FWIP
And when we get done, you HAVE to sleep. Promise?
SLUURP
Sleep. Pah! Overrated!
I don't need it! Besides, "there's something on my foot!"
Let's go!

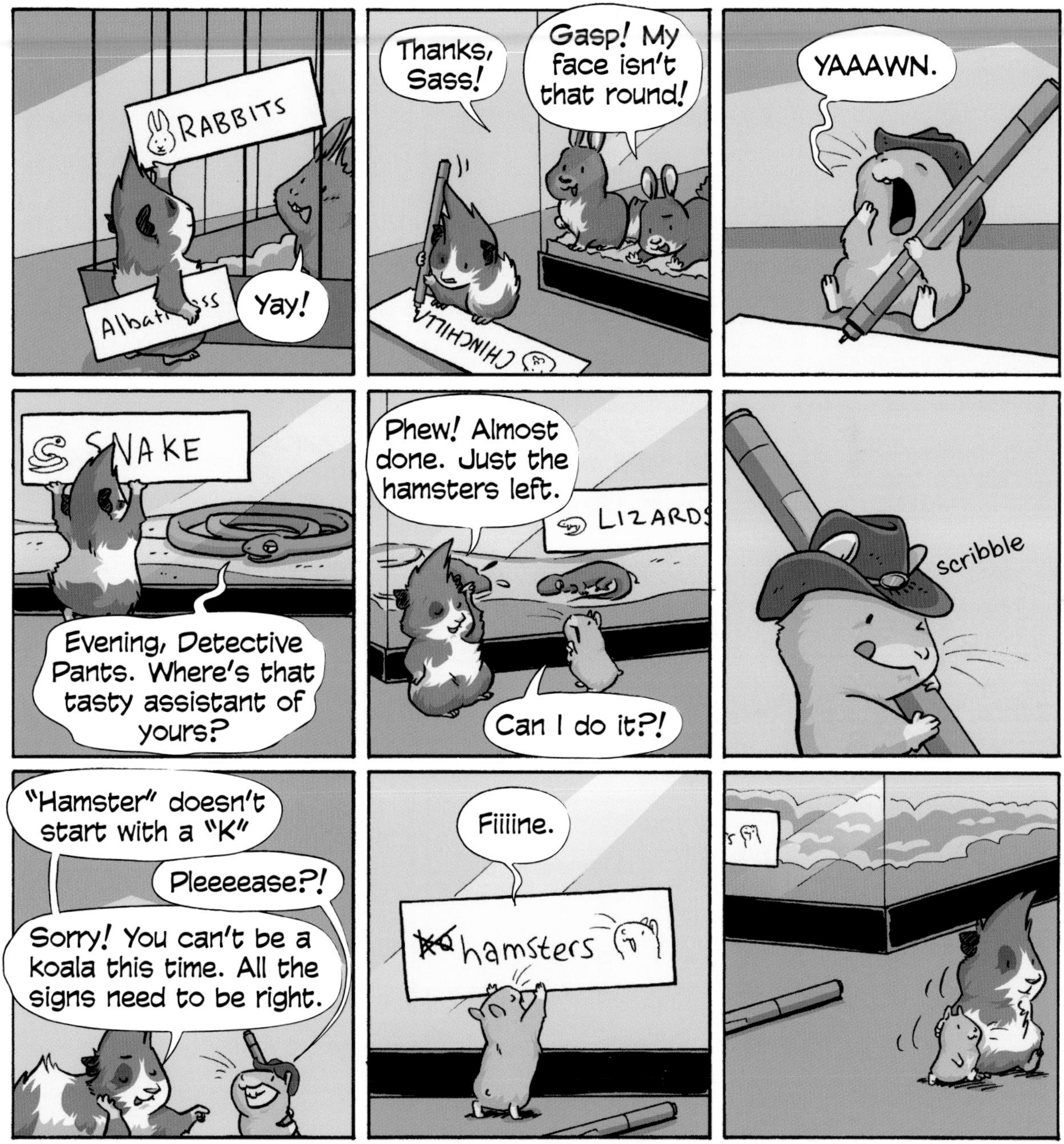
RABBITS
Albat ss
Yay!
Thanks, Sass!
Gasp! My face isn't that round!
CHINCHILLA
YAAAWN.
SNAKE
Evening, Detective Pants. Where's that tasty assistant of yours?
Phew! Almost done. Just the hamsters left.
LIZARDS
Can I do it?!
scribble
"Hamster" doesn't start with a "K"
Pleeeease?!
Sorry! You can't be a koala this time. All the signs need to be right.
Fiiiine.
hamsters

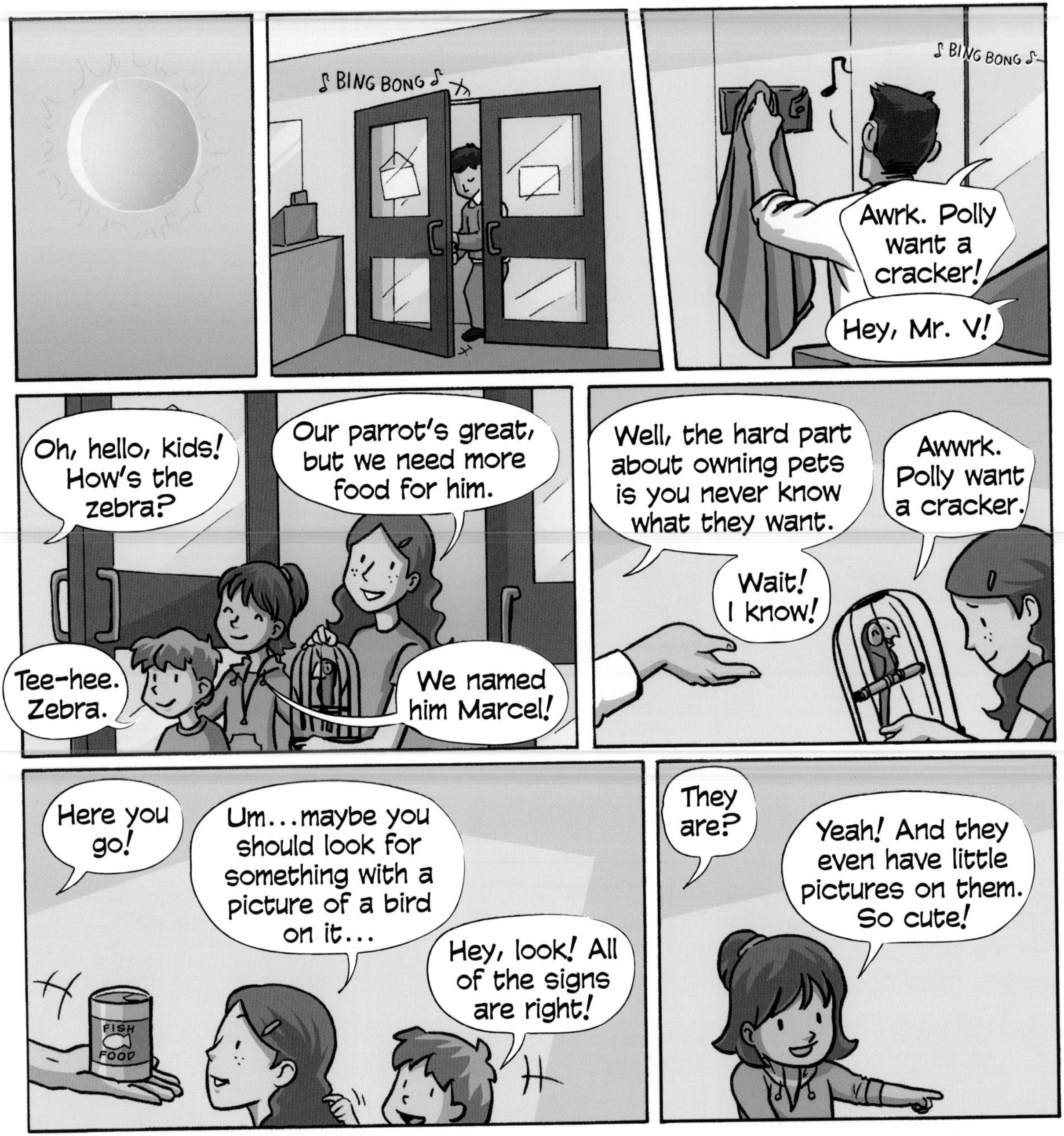
BING BONG
BING BONG
Awrk. Polly want a cracker!
Hey, Mr. V!
Oh, hello, kids! How's the zebra?
Our parrot's great, but we need more food for him.
Tee-hee. Zebra.
We named him Marcel!
Well, the hard part about owning pets is you never know what they want.
Awwrk. Polly want a cracker.
Wait! I know!
Here you go!
Um...maybe you should look for something with a picture of a bird on it...
FISH FOOD
Hey, look! All of the signs are right!
They are?
Yeah! And they even have little pictures on them. So cute!

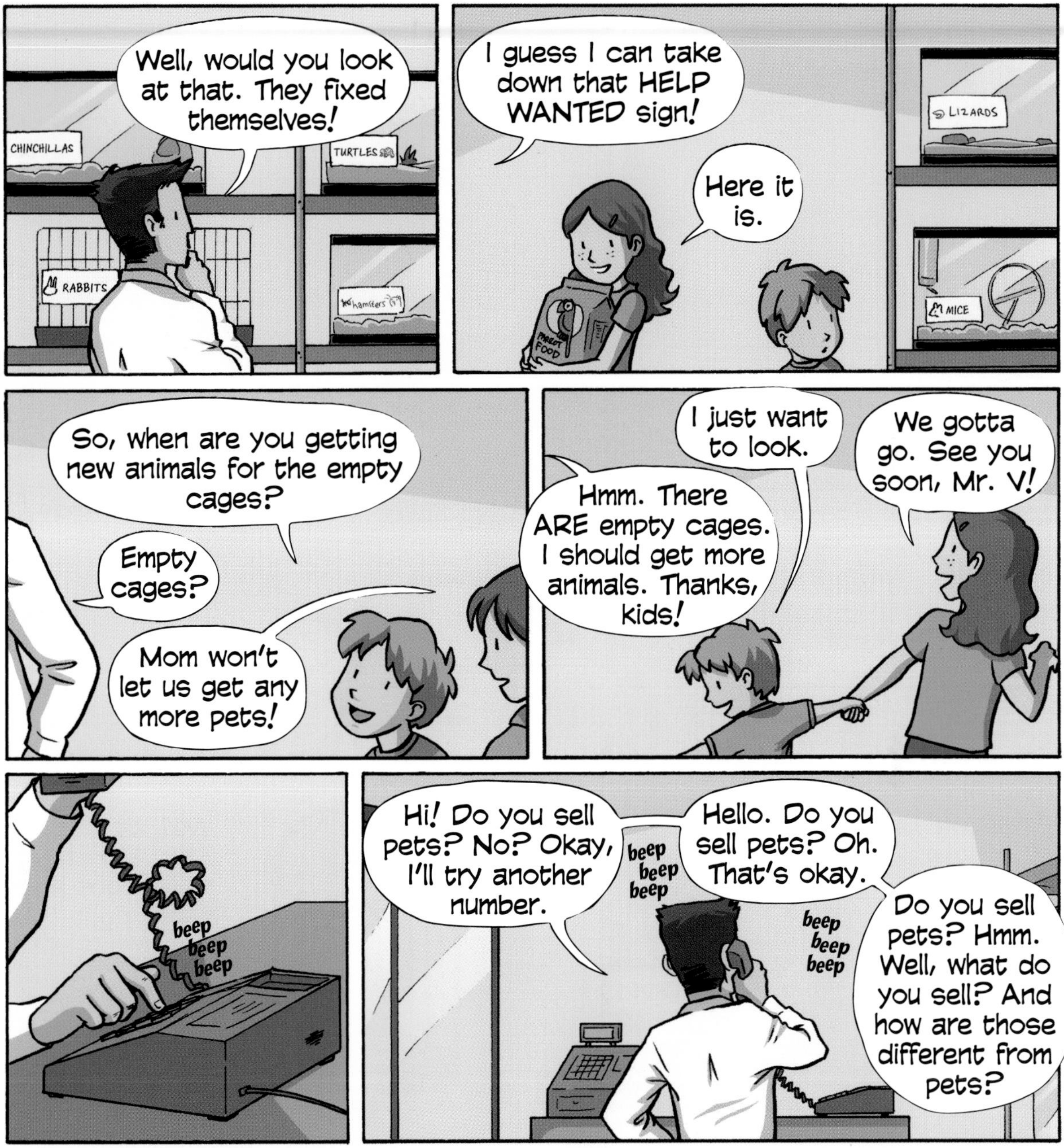
Well, would you look at that. They fixed themselves!
CHINCHILLAS
TURTLES
RABBITS
hamsters
I guess I can take down that HELP WANTED sign!
Here it is.
LIZARDS
MICE
PARROT FOOD
So, when are you getting new animals for the empty cages?
Empty cages?
Mom won't let us get any more pets!
Hmm. There ARE empty cages. I should get more animals. Thanks, kids!
I just want to look.
We gotta go. See you soon, Mr. V!
beep beep beep
Hi! Do you sell pets? No? Okay, I'll try another number.
beep beep beep
Hello. Do you sell pets? Oh. That's okay.
beep beep beep
Do you sell pets? Hmm. Well, what do you sell? And how are those different from pets?

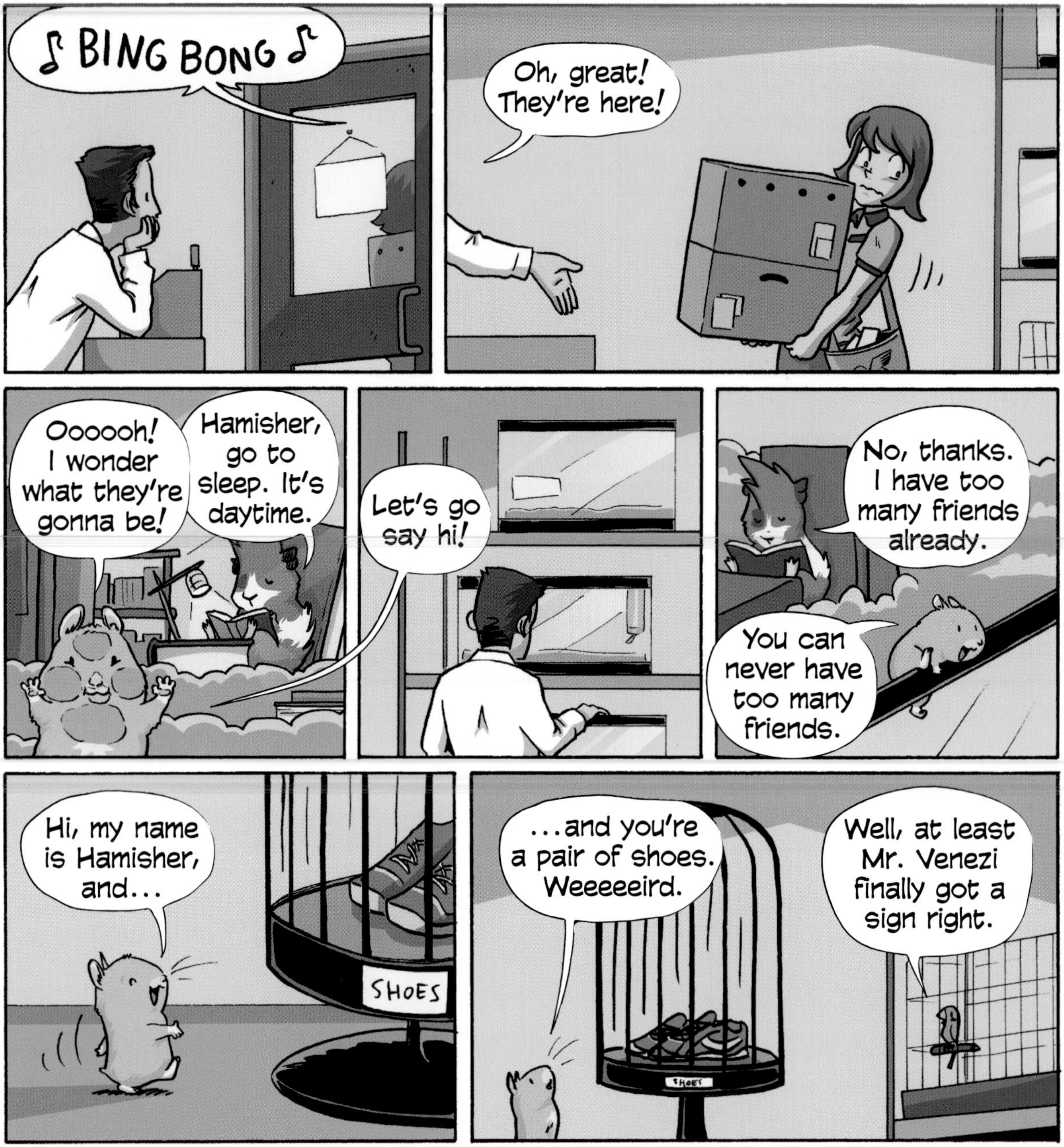
♪ BING BONG ♪
Oh, great! They're here!
Oooooh! I wonder what they're gonna be!
Hamisher, go to sleep. It's daytime.
Let's go say hi!
No, thanks. I have too many friends already.
You can never have too many friends.
Hi, my name is Hamisher, and...
SHOES
...and you're a pair of shoes. Weeeeeird.
Well, at least Mr. Venezi finally got a sign right.

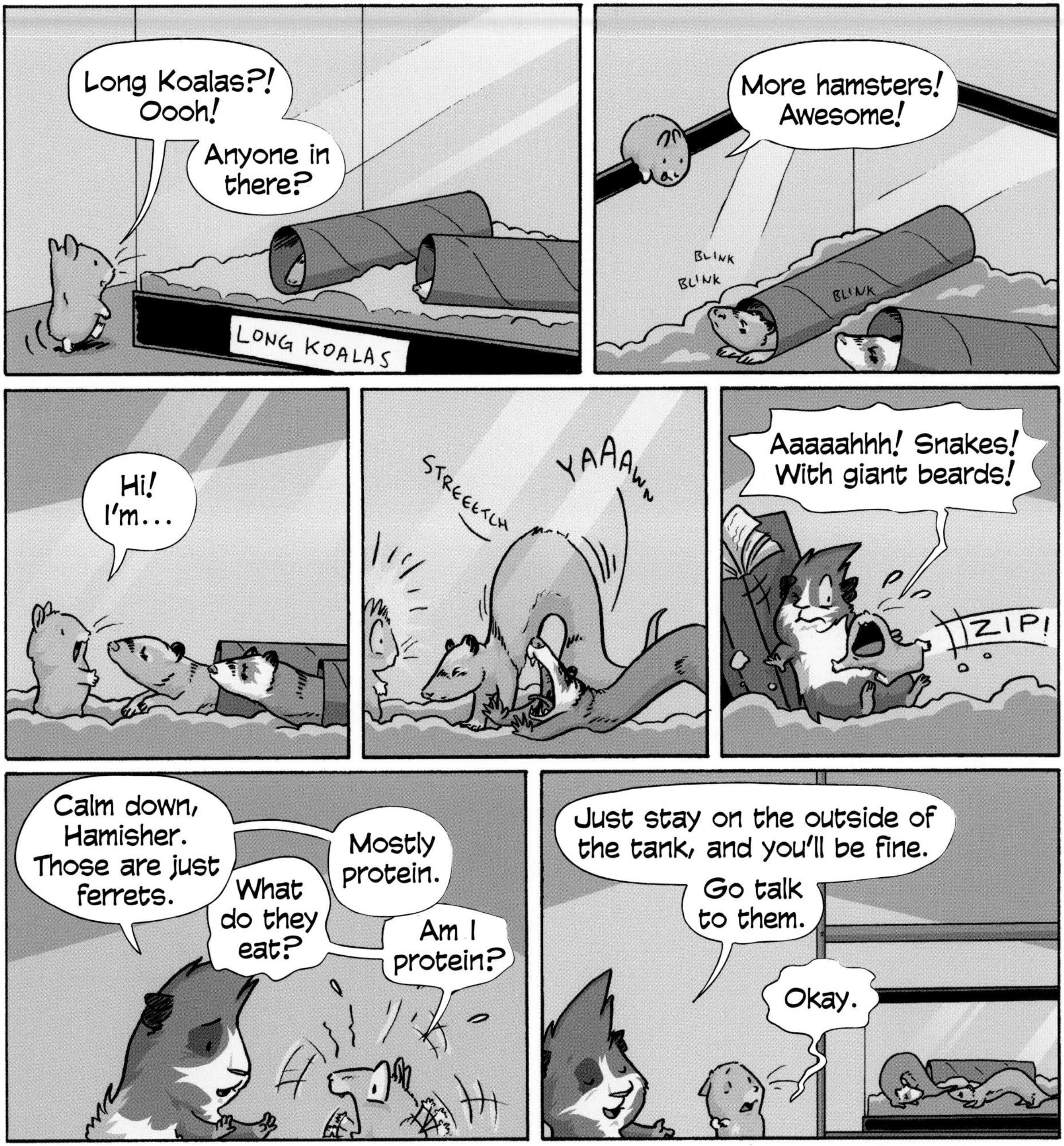
Long Koalas?! Oooh!
Anyone in there?
LONG KOALAS
More hamsters! Awesome!
BLINK
BLINK
BLINK
Hi! I'm...
STREEETCH
YAAAWN
Aaaaahhh! Snakes! With giant beards!
ZIP!
Calm down, Hamisher. Those are just ferrets.
What do they eat?
Mostly protein.
Am I protein?
Just stay on the outside of the tank, and you'll be fine.
Go talk to them.
Okay.

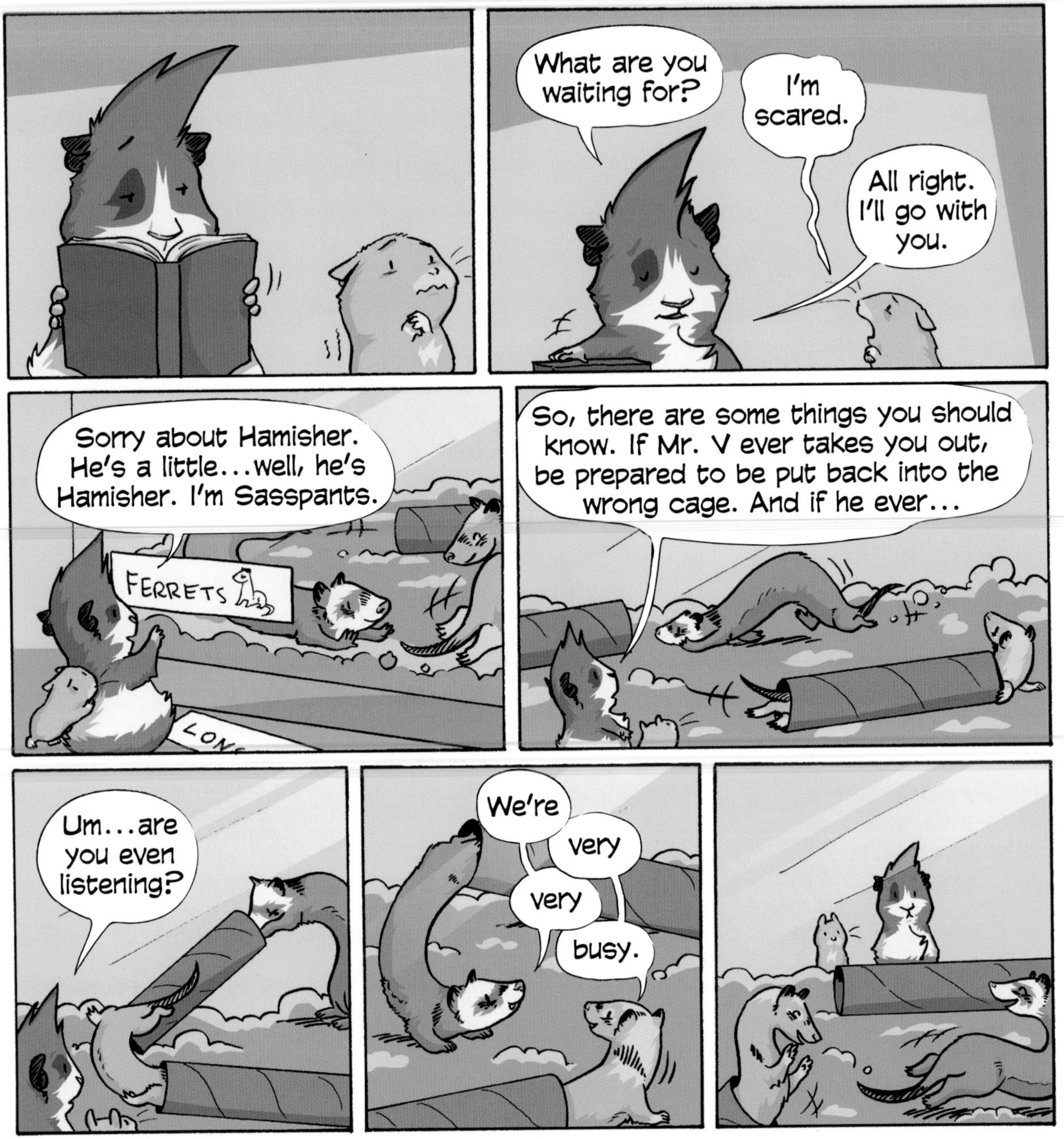
What are you waiting for?
I'm scared.
All right. I'll go with you.
Sorry about Hamisher. He's a little...well, he's Hamisher. I'm Sasspants.
FERRETS
LONG
So, there are some things you should know. If Mr. V ever takes you out, be prepared to be put back into the wrong cage. And if he ever...
Um...are you even listening?
We're
very
very
busy.

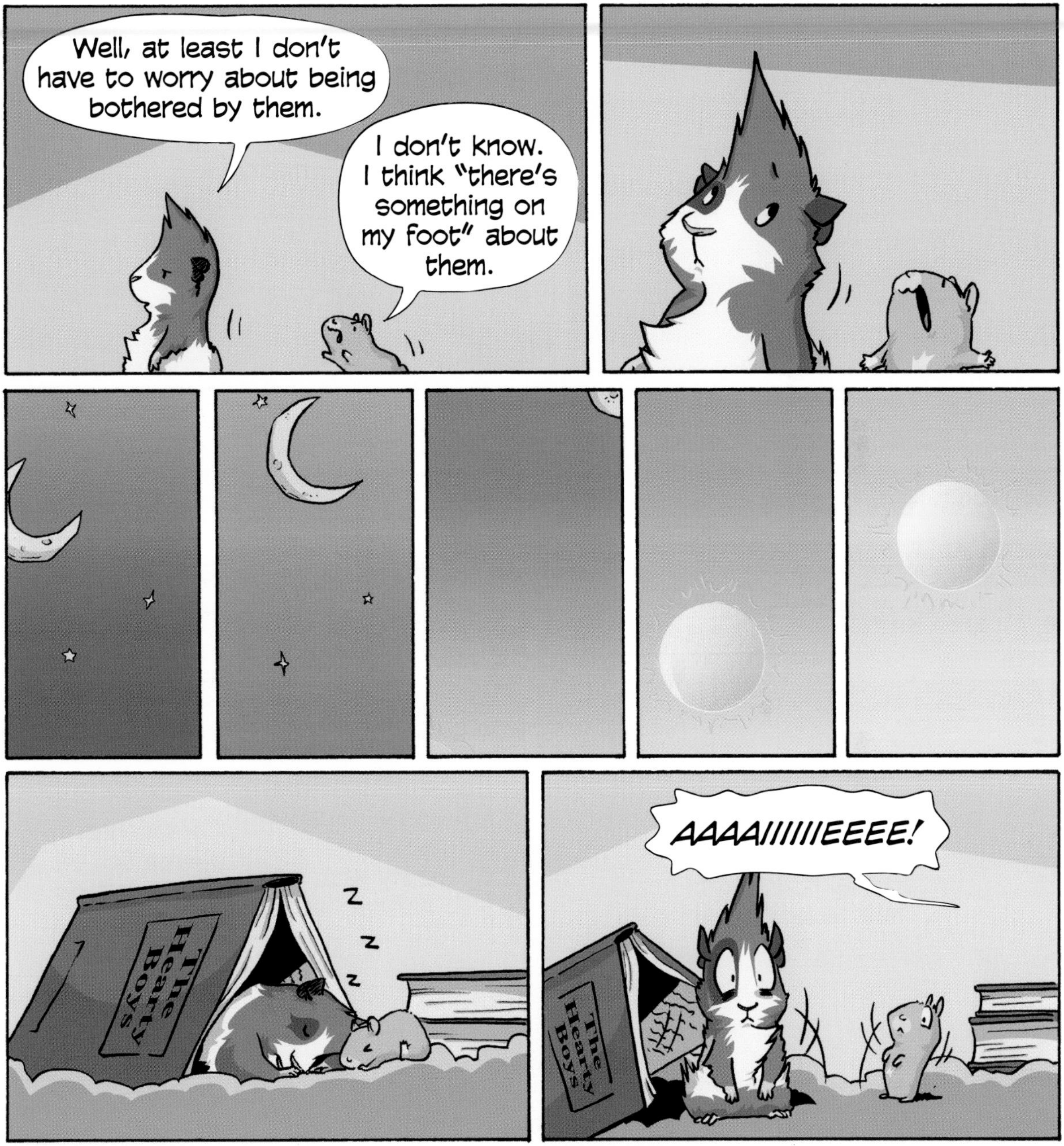
Well, at least I don't have to worry about being bothered by them.
I don't know. I think "there's something on my foot" about them.
The Hearty Boys
Z Z Z
AAAAIIIIIIIEEEE!
The Hearty Boys

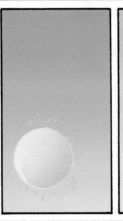

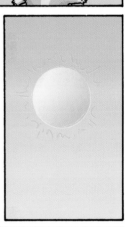

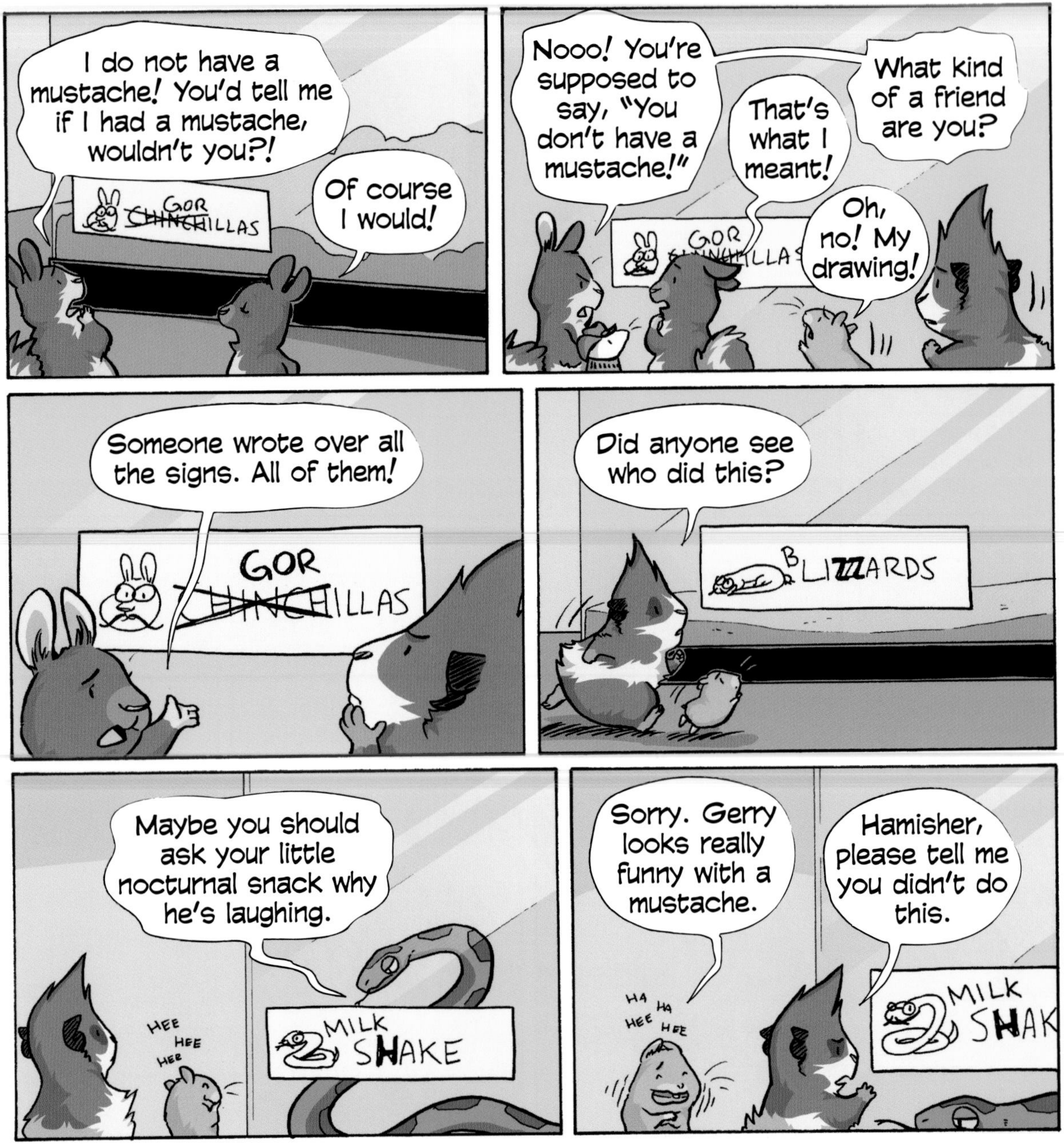
I do not have a mustache! You'd tell me if I had a mustache, wouldn't you?!
GOR CHINCHILLAS
Of course I would!
Nooo! You're supposed to say, "You don't have a mustache!"
What kind of a friend are you?
That's what I meant!
Oh, no! My drawing!
Someone wrote over all the signs. All of them!
GOR CHINCHILLAS
Did anyone see who did this?
BLIZZARDS
Maybe you should ask your little nocturnal snack why he's laughing.
HEE HEE HEE
MILK SHAKE
Sorry. Gerry looks really funny with a mustache.
Hamisher, please tell me you didn't do this.
HA HA HEE HEE

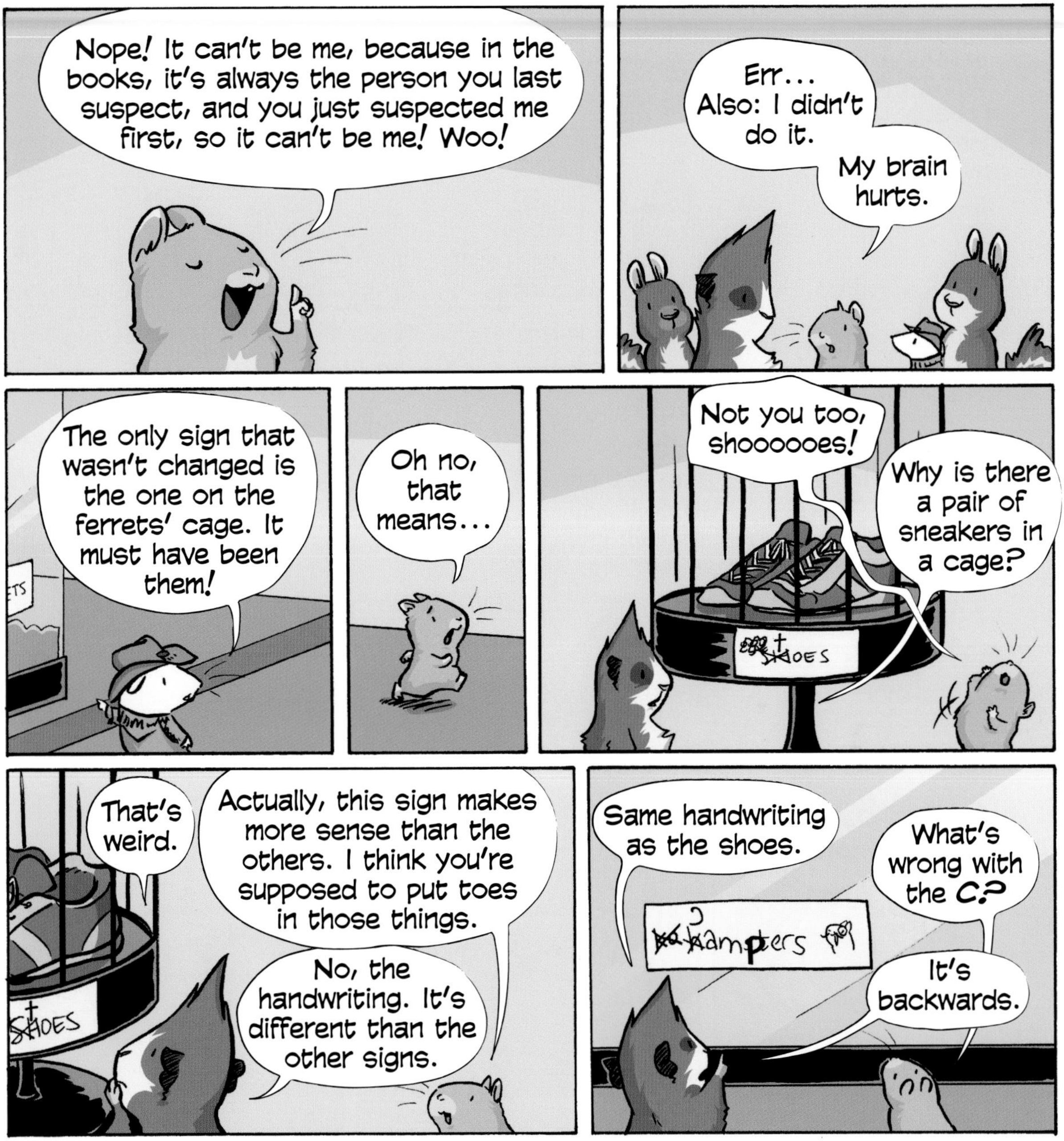
Nope! It can't be me, because in the books, it's always the person you last suspect, and you just suspected me first, so it can't be me! Woo!
Err... Also: I didn't do it.
My brain hurts.
The only sign that wasn't changed is the one on the ferrets' cage. It must have been them!
Oh no, that means...
Not you too, shoooooes!
Why is there a pair of sneakers in a cage?
That's weird.
Actually, this sign makes more sense than the others. I think you're supposed to put toes in those things.
No, the handwriting. It's different than the other signs.
Same handwriting as the shoes.
What's wrong with the C?
It's backwards.

Oooh! The campers were probably up all night. I bet they saw who did it!

Good thinking.

Hey!

Hi!

Happy Birthday!

Who is it? I can't see. The sun is in my eyes.

The SUN?!

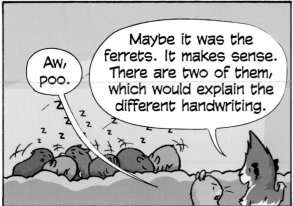

Aw, poo.

Maybe it was the ferrets. It makes sense. There are two of them, which would explain the different handwriting.

I don't think they should be allowed to drink any more soda either.

Okay, you two. I've got some questions.

Can't talk now

too much

to do. So busy.

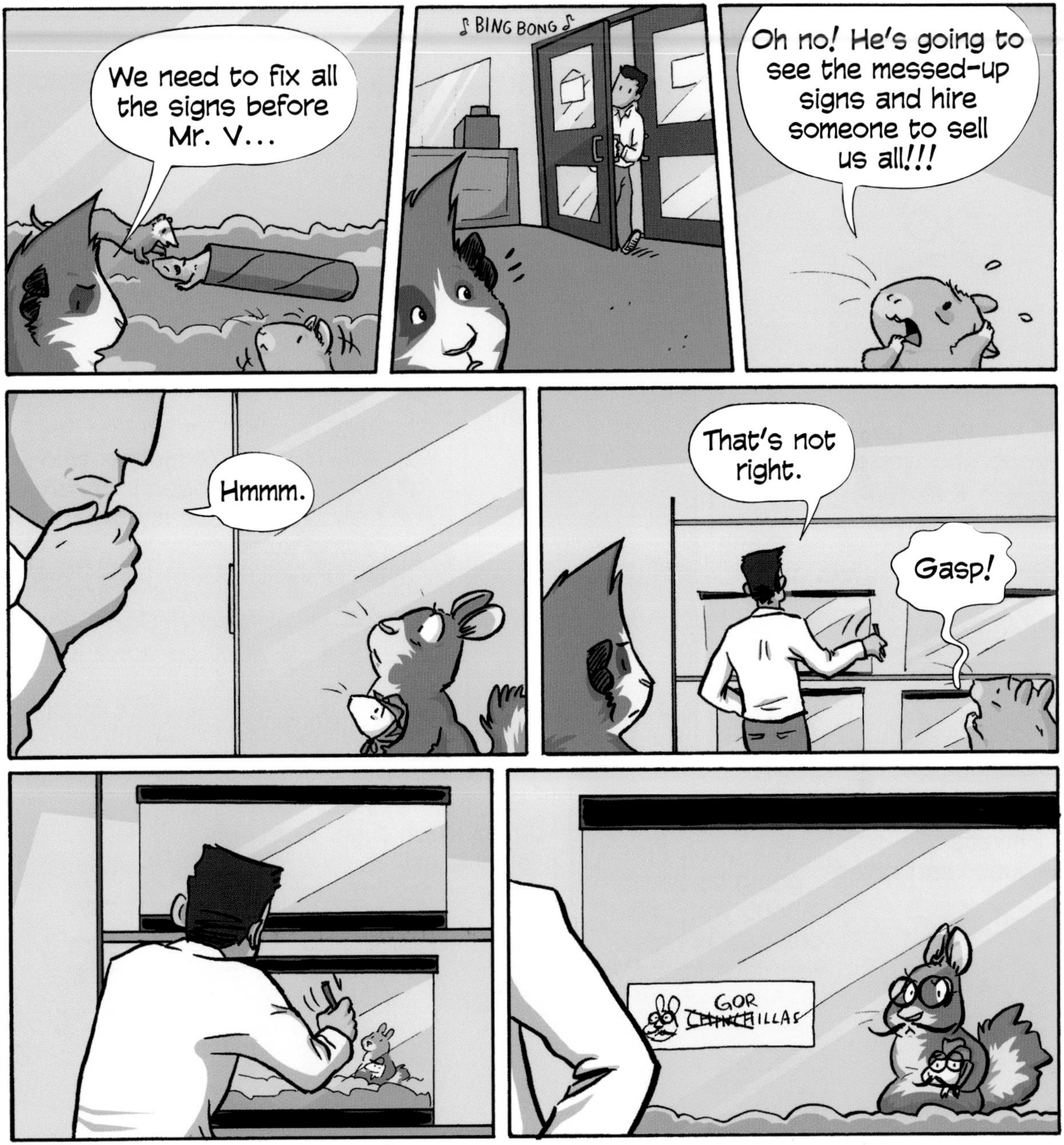
We need to fix all the signs before Mr. V...
BING BONG
Oh no! He's going to see the messed-up signs and hire someone to sell us all!!!
Hmmm.
That's not right.
Gasp!
GOR
CHINCHILLAS

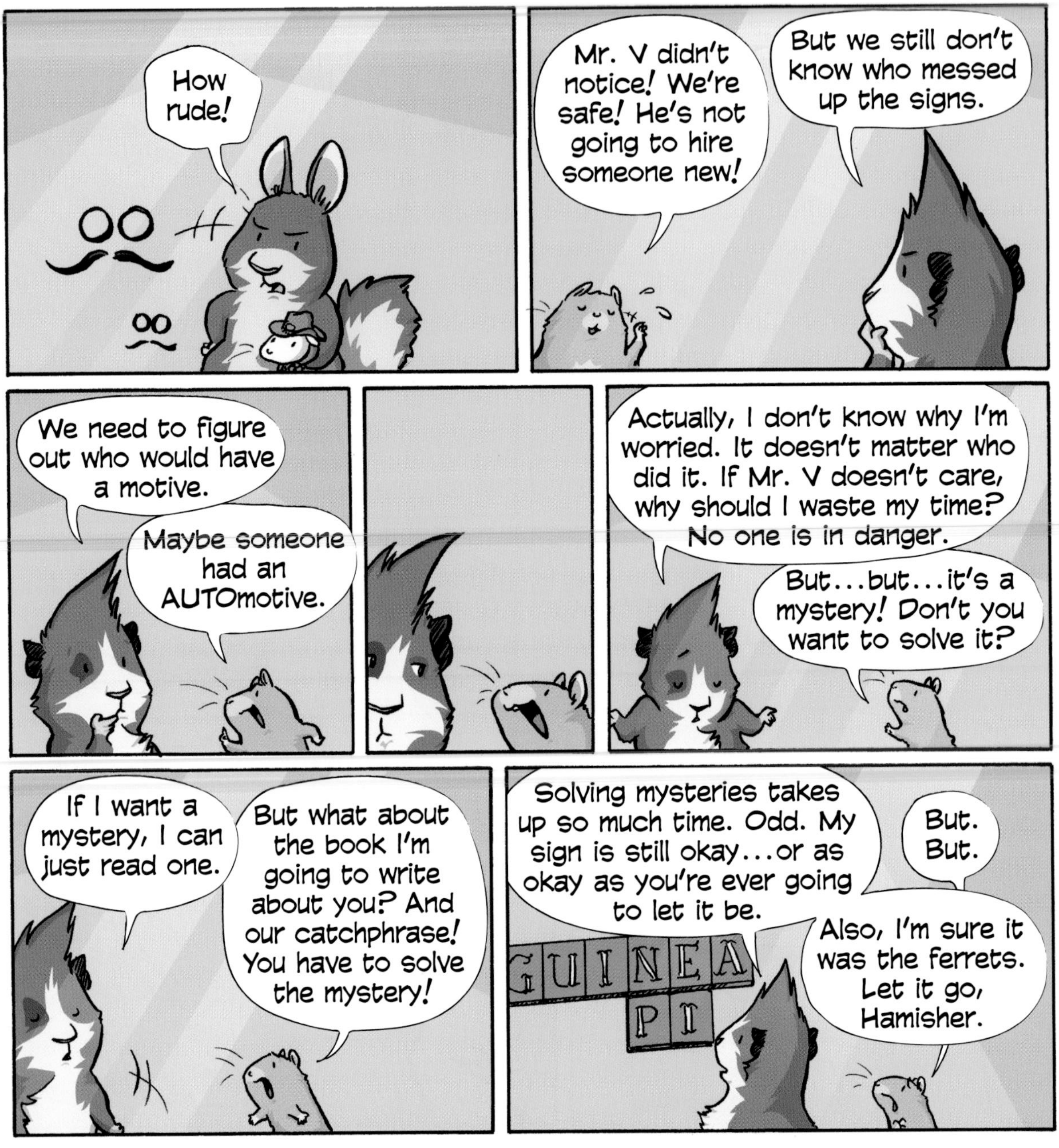
How rude!
Mr. V didn't notice! We're safe! He's not going to hire someone new!
But we still don't know who messed up the signs.
We need to figure out who would have a motive.
Maybe someone had an AUTOmotive.
Actually, I don't know why I'm worried. It doesn't matter who did it. If Mr. V doesn't care, why should I waste my time? No one is in danger.
But...but...it's a mystery! Don't you want to solve it?
If I want a mystery, I can just read one.
But what about the book I'm going to write about you? And our catchphrase! You have to solve the mystery!
Solving mysteries takes up so much time. Odd. My sign is still okay...or as okay as you're ever going to let it be.
But. But.
Also, I'm sure it was the ferrets. Let it go, Hamisher.
GUINEA
PI

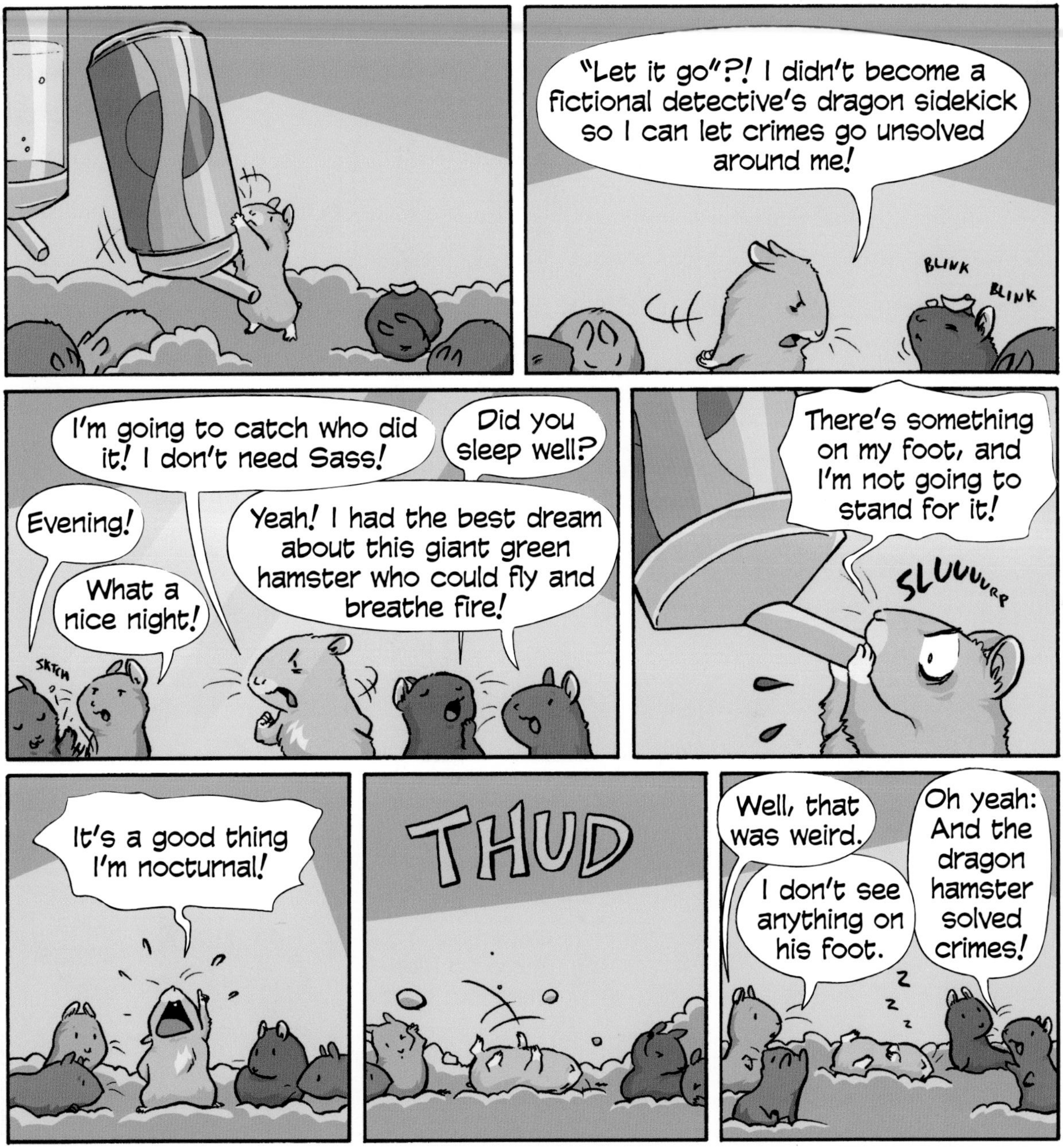
"Let it go"?! I didn't become a fictional detective's dragon sidekick so I can let crimes go unsolved around me!
BLINK
BLINK
I'm going to catch who did it! I don't need Sass!
Did you sleep well?
Evening!
Yeah! I had the best dream about this giant green hamster who could fly and breathe fire!
What a nice night!
SKTCH
There's something on my foot, and I'm not going to stand for it!
SLUUUURP
It's a good thing I'm nocturnal!
THUD
Well, that was weird.
I don't see anything on his foot.
Oh yeah: And the dragon hamster solved crimes!
Z
Z
Z

Not again!!!

GODZ ~~CHINCHILLAS~~ ILLAS

Ah, lovely. Always nice to be reminded I have no hands.

Godzillas?! This is even worse than the last one!

Sass! Come quick!

HAND ~~RATS~~ SNAKES

GODZ ~~CHINCHILLAS~~

Let me guess. All the signs were changed, except the ferrets?

RUB RUB

Did you see who did it?

Do you think we'd be this upset if we knew who did it?!

There's still an hour before Mr. V comes in. I'll fix the signs.

That's evidence! You have to keep them like that.

What I have to do is make sure Mr. V doesn't hire anyone new to come and fix the signs. The ferrets are just playing tricks.

Why are you so sure it's the ferrets?

Well, for one, the signs are up high, so the culprits have to be tall. AND there are two different handwritings, which means two people are working together. AND the ferrets' sign is the only one not being vandalized. AND they don't seem interested in making friends.

That settles it! The ferrets didn't do it!

Um, were you listening to what I just said?

In your mystery books, it's never the person who looks like they did it!!

SHOES

TTS

RAMPES

Sorry, Ham, but sometimes life isn't like in the books. I'm going to tell the ferrets they have to stop.

KN
XISH

Oof.

Here, let me get that.

There! All done.

FINCHES

GRINCH

Okay, listen up... um... I don't even know your names.

Wadsworth.

Too... busy... sorry.

I know you're the ones changing the signs. That needs to stop NOW. I mean it.

I know you didn't do it, Wadsworth and Toobusy! Tell her you didn't do it!

27

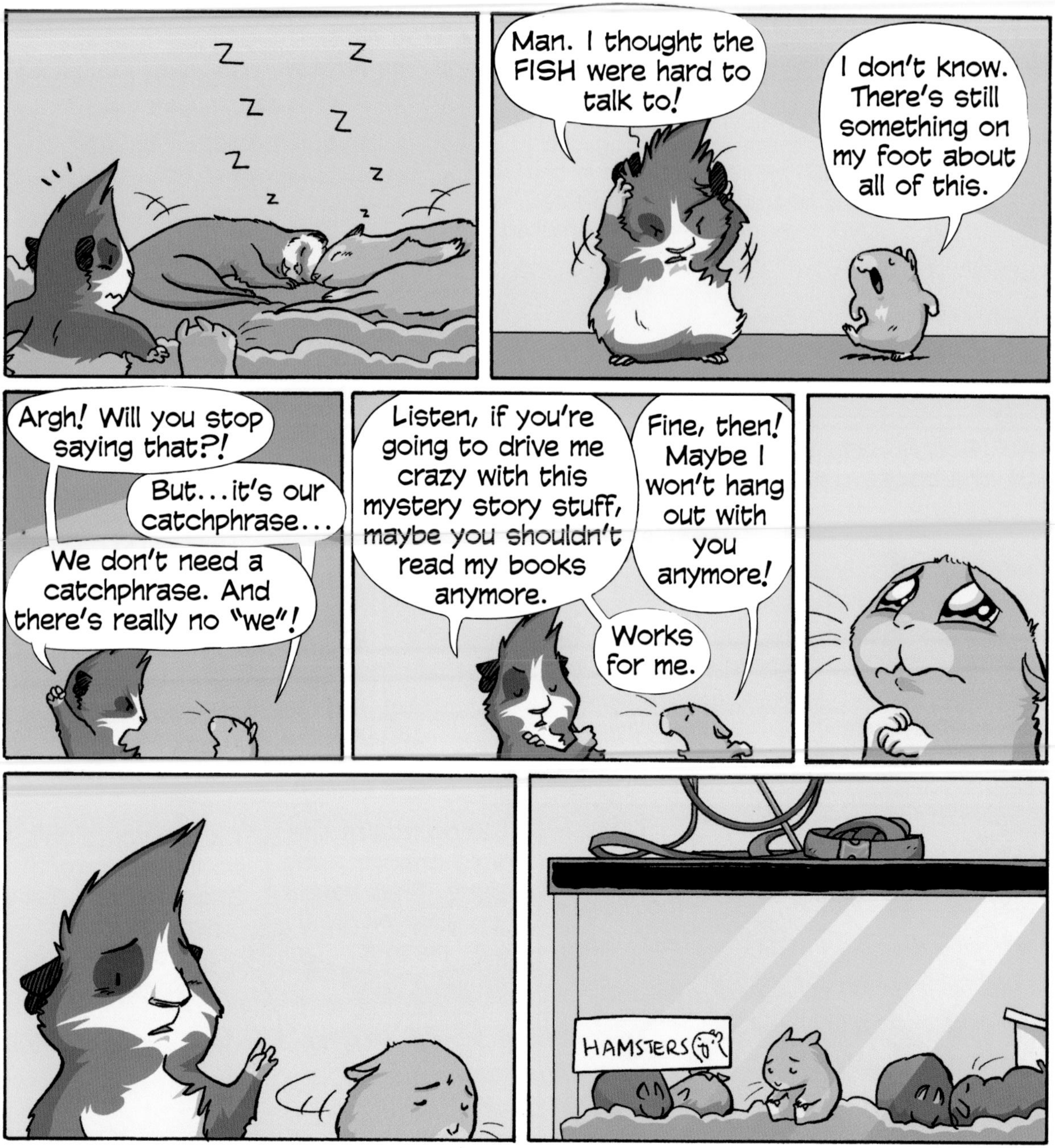
Z Z Z Z Z Z z z
Man. I thought the FISH were hard to talk to!
I don't know. There's still something on my foot about all of this.
Argh! Will you stop saying that?!
But...it's our catchphrase...
We don't need a catchphrase. And there's really no "we"!
Listen, if you're going to drive me crazy with this mystery story stuff, maybe you shouldn't read my books anymore.
Fine, then! Maybe I won't hang out with you anymore!
Works for me.
HAMSTERS

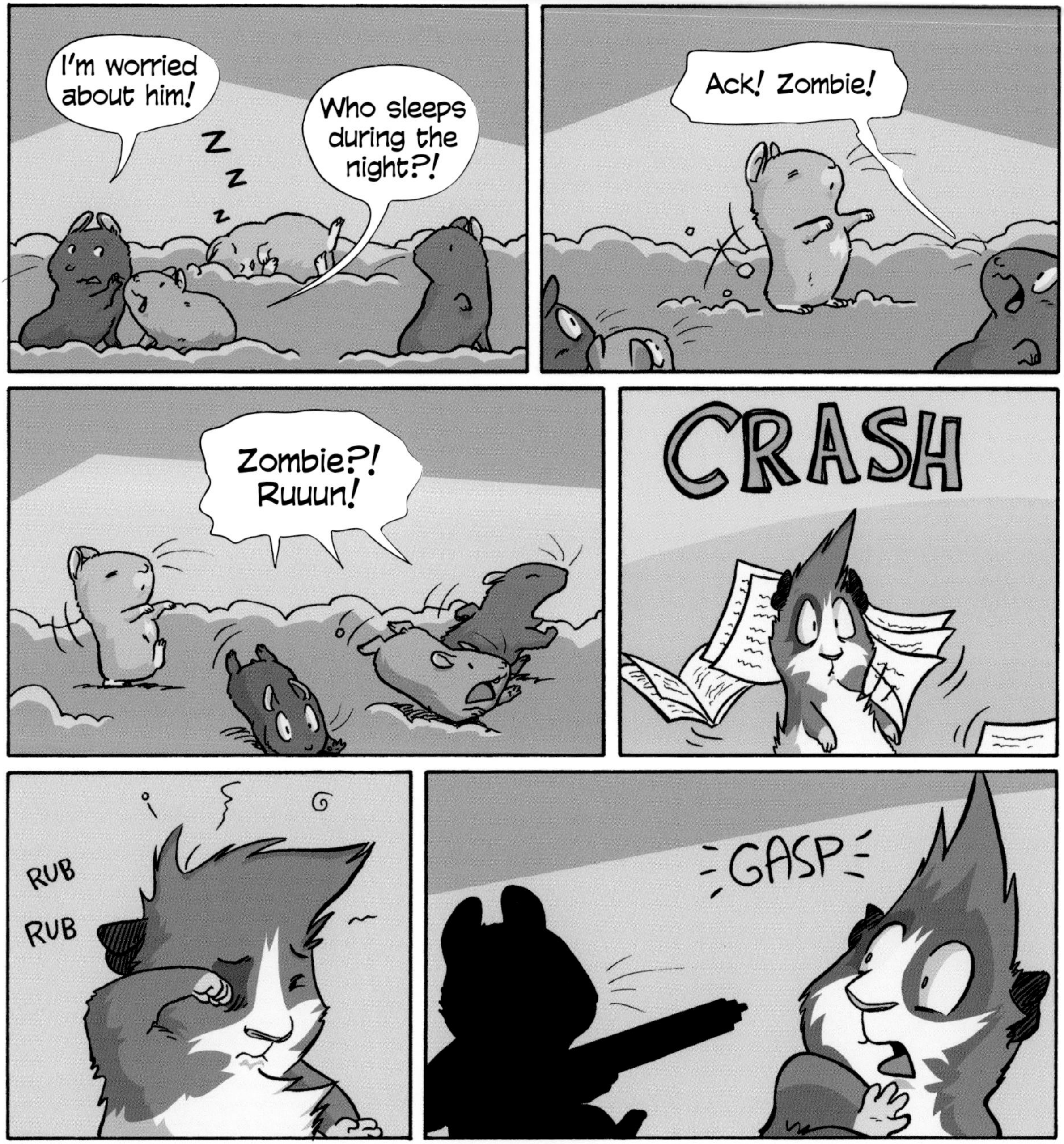
I'm worried about him!
Z Z Z
Who sleeps during the night?!
Ack! Zombie!
Zombie?! Ruuun!
CRASH
RUB
RUB
GASP

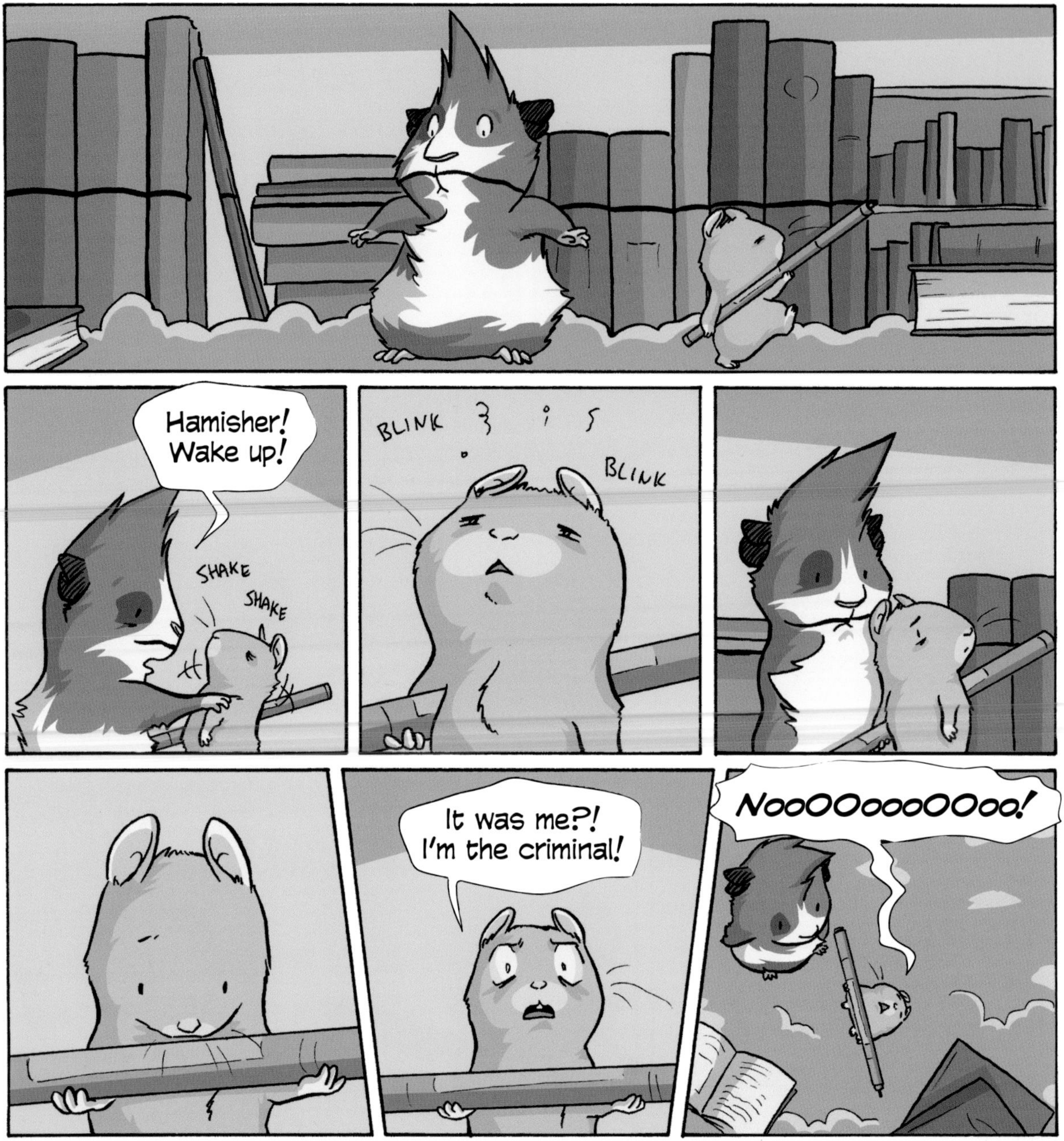
Hamisher! Wake up!
SHAKE
SHAKE
BLINK
BLINK
It was me?! I'm the criminal!
NooOOoooOOoo!

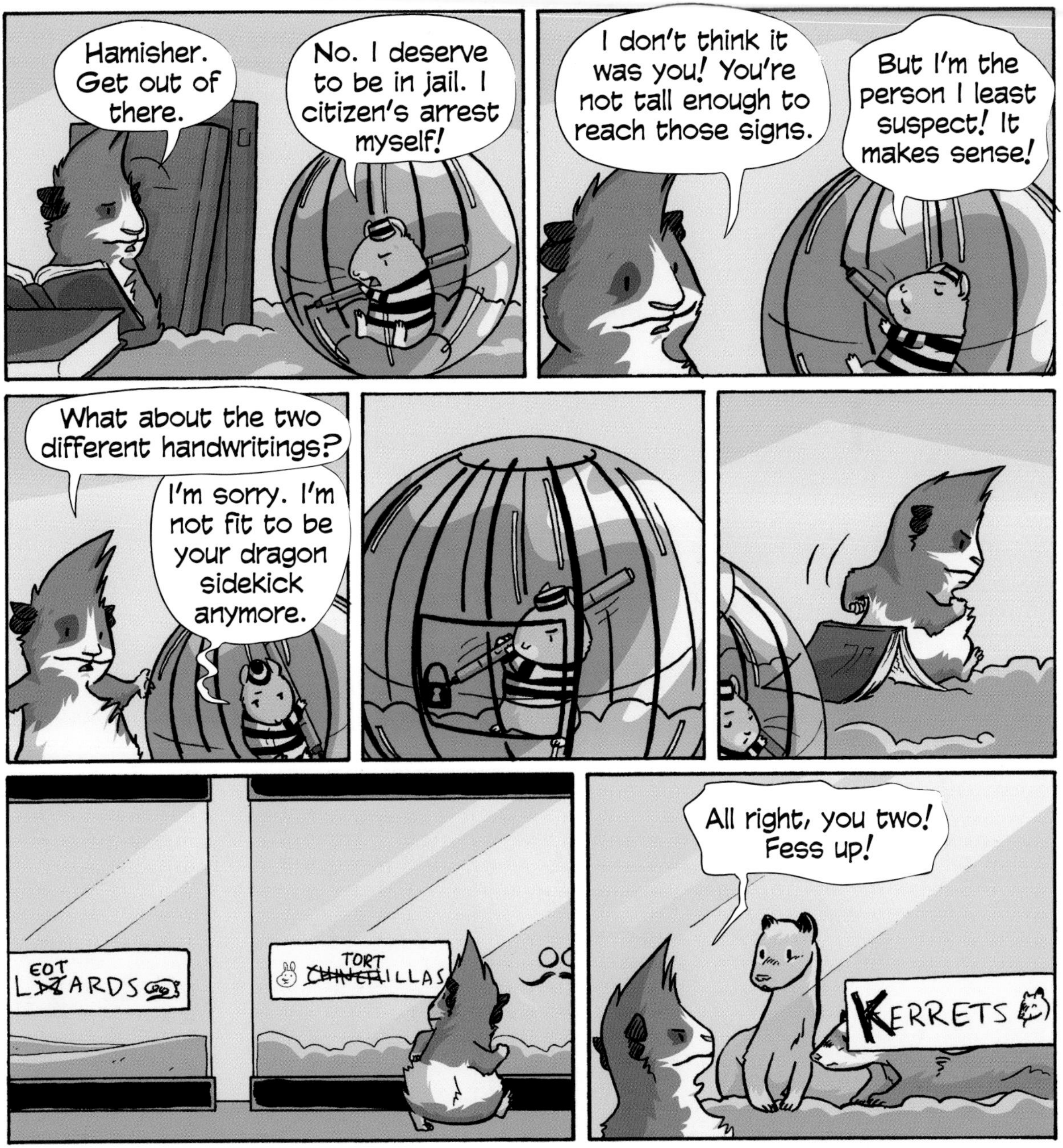
Hamisher. Get out of there.
No. I deserve to be in jail. I citizen's arrest myself!
I don't think it was you! You're not tall enough to reach those signs.
But I'm the person I least suspect! It makes sense!
What about the two different handwritings?
I'm sorry. I'm not fit to be your dragon sidekick anymore.
EOT
L~~IZ~~ARDS
TORT
~~CHINCH~~ILLAS
All right, you two! Fess up!
KERRETS

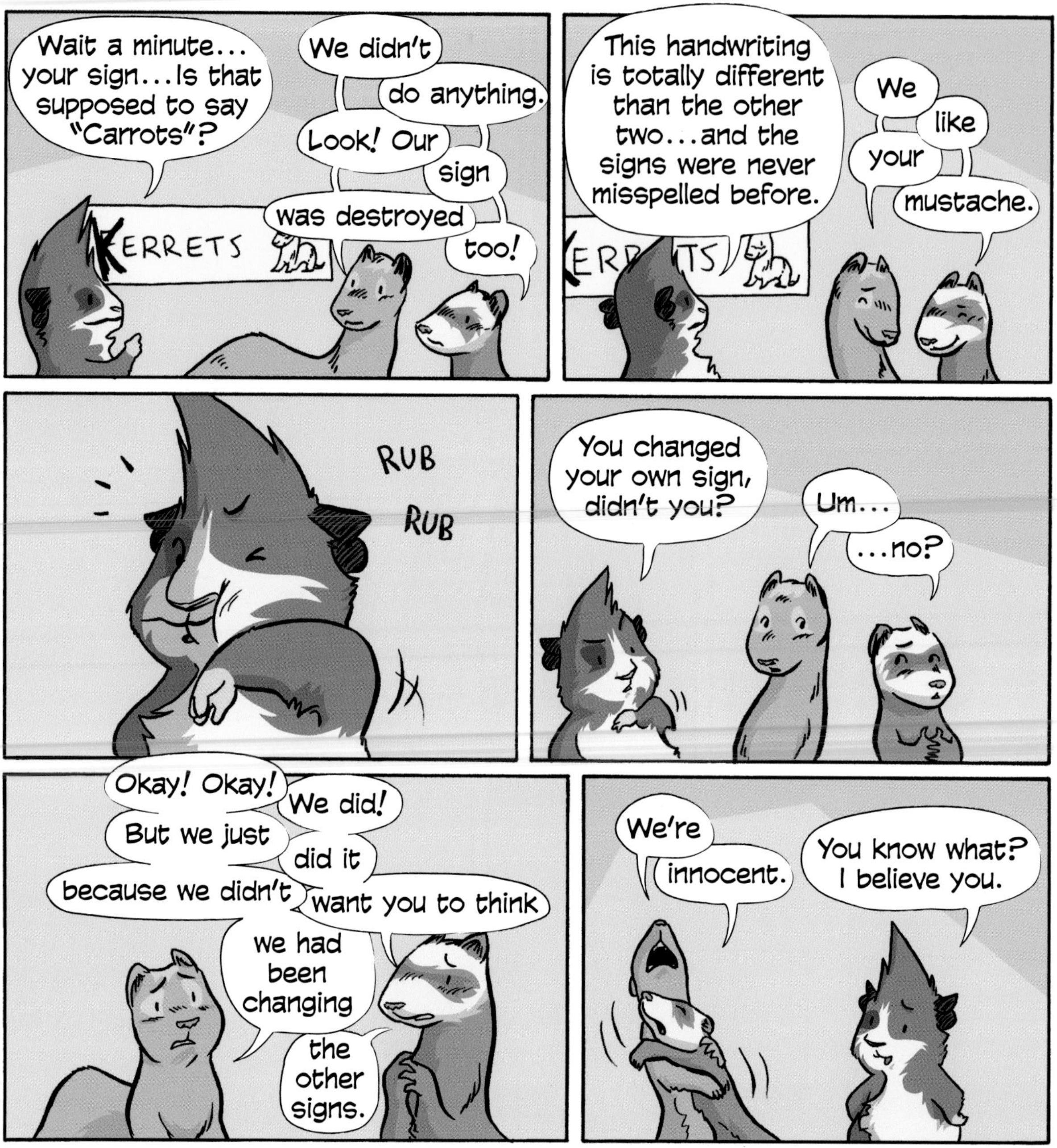
Wait a minute... your sign... Is that supposed to say "Carrots"?
KERRETS
We didn't
do anything.
Look! Our
sign
was destroyed
too!
This handwriting is totally different than the other two... and the signs were never misspelled before.
We
like
your
mustache.
RUB
RUB
You changed your own sign, didn't you?
Um...
...no?
Okay! Okay!
We did!
But we just
did it
because we didn't
want you to think
we had been changing
the other signs.
We're
innocent.
You know what? I believe you.

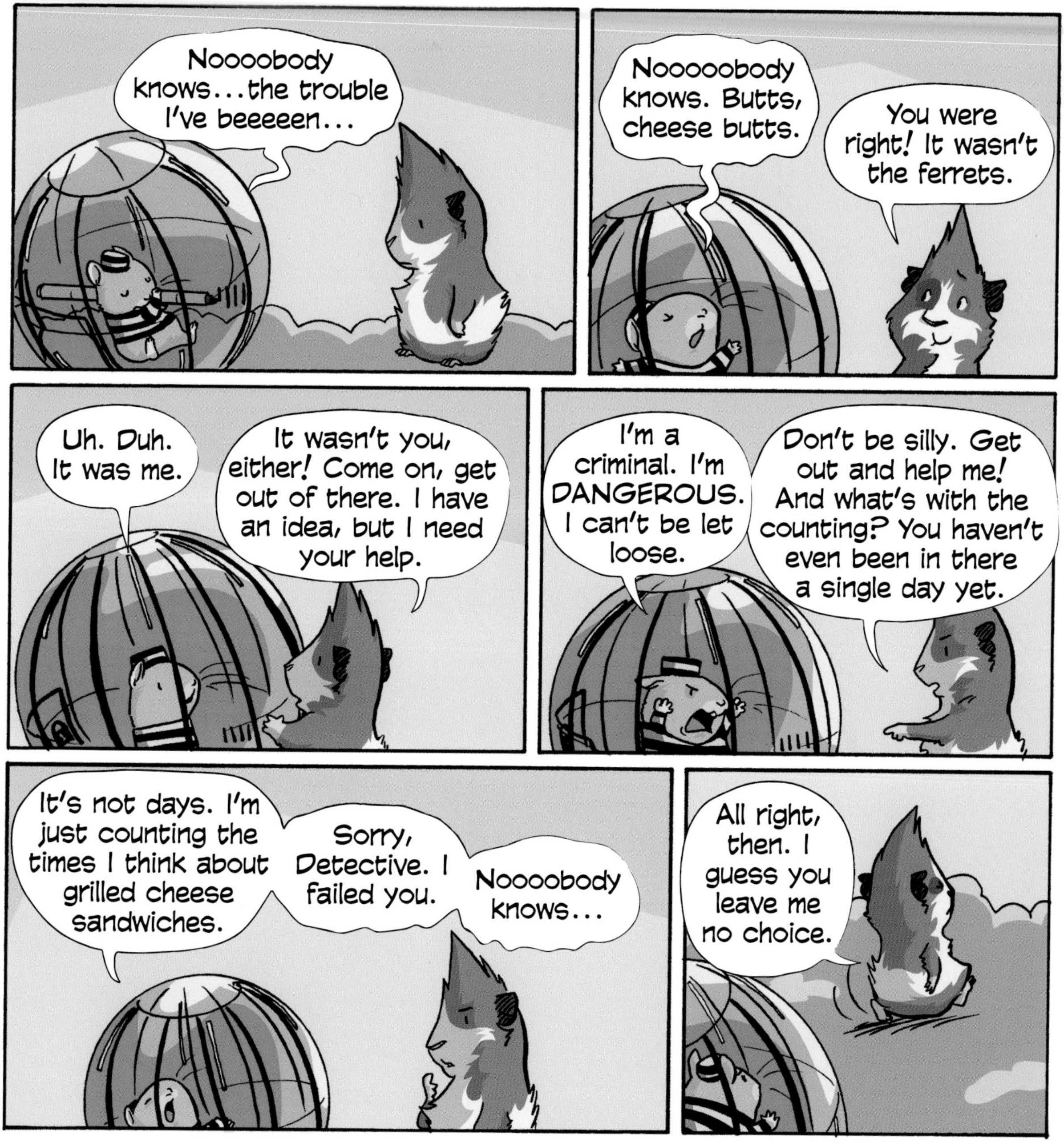
Nooooobody knows...the trouble I've beeeeen...
Noooooobody knows. Butts, cheese butts.
You were right! It wasn't the ferrets.
Uh. Duh. It was me.
It wasn't you, either! Come on, get out of there. I have an idea, but I need your help.
I'm a criminal. I'm DANGEROUS. I can't be let loose.
Don't be silly. Get out and help me! And what's with the counting? You haven't even been in there a single day yet.
It's not days. I'm just counting the times I think about grilled cheese sandwiches.
Sorry, Detective. I failed you.
Nooooobody knows...
All right, then. I guess you leave me no choice.

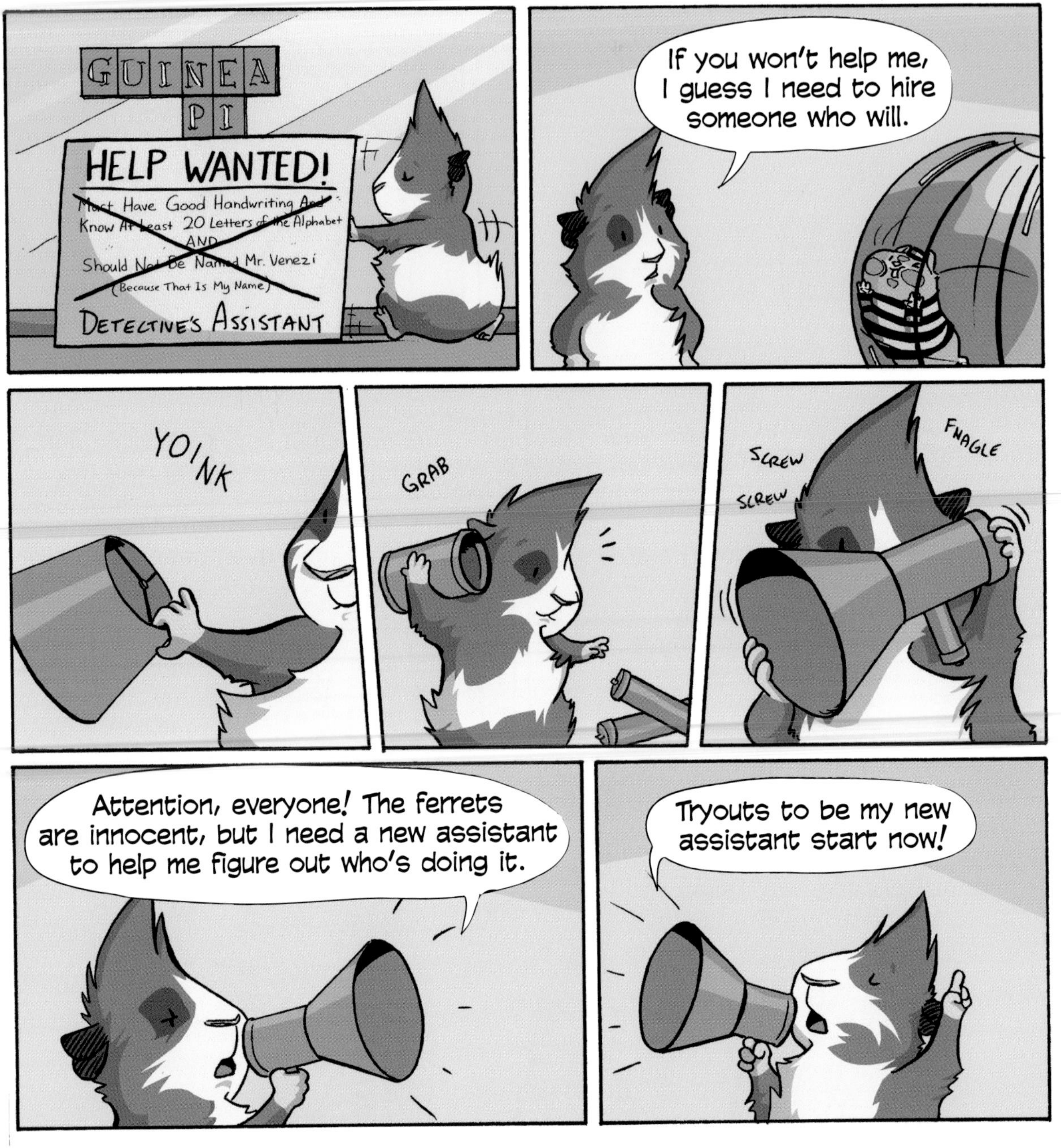
GUINEA PI
HELP WANTED!
Must Have Good Handwriting And Know At Least 20 Letters of the Alphabet
AND
Should Not Be Named Mr. Venezi (Because That Is My Name)
DETECTIVE'S ASSISTANT
If you won't help me, I guess I need to hire someone who will.
YOINK
GRAB
SCREW
SCREW
FNAGLE
Attention, everyone! The ferrets are innocent, but I need a new assistant to help me figure out who's doing it.
Tryouts to be my new assistant start now!

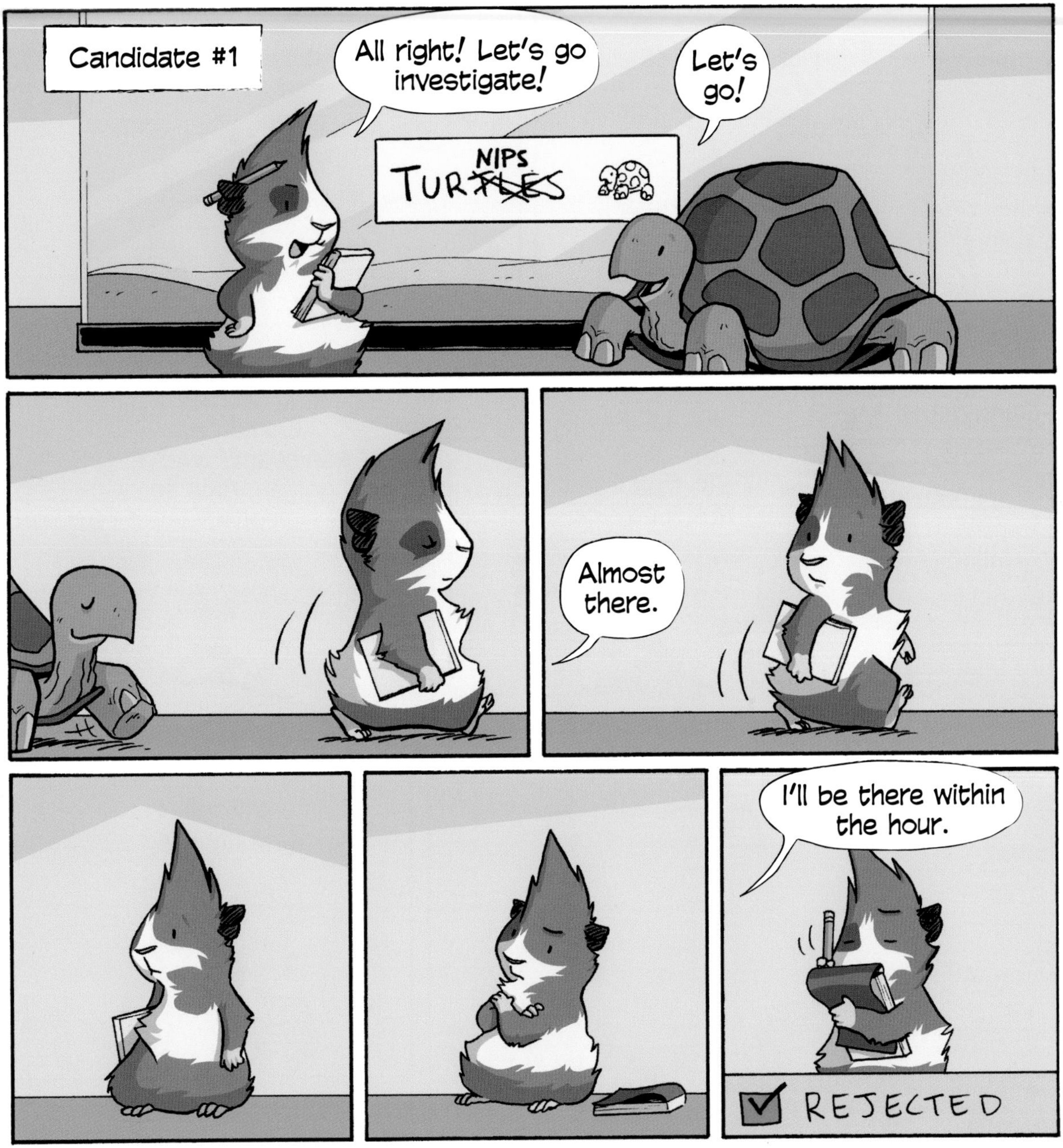
Candidate #1
All right! Let's go investigate!
Let's go!
TURNIPS
Almost there.
I'll be there within the hour.
REJECTED

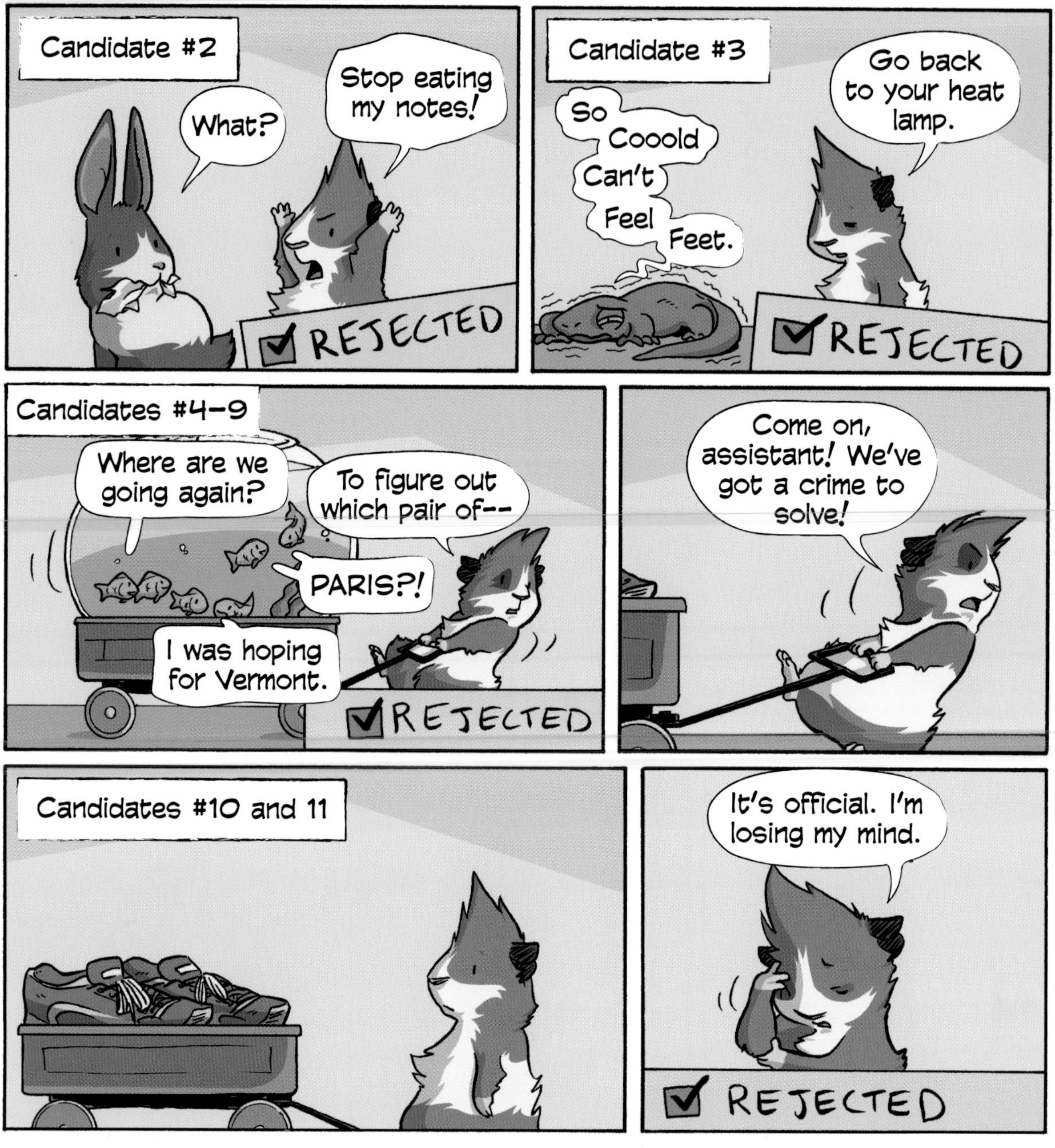
Candidate #2
What?
Stop eating my notes!
REJECTED
Candidate #3
So Cooold Can't Feel Feet.
Go back to your heat lamp.
REJECTED
Candidates #4–9
Where are we going again?
To figure out which pair of--
PARIS?!
I was hoping for Vermont.
REJECTED
Come on, assistant! We've got a crime to solve!
Candidates #10 and 11
It's official. I'm losing my mind.
REJECTED

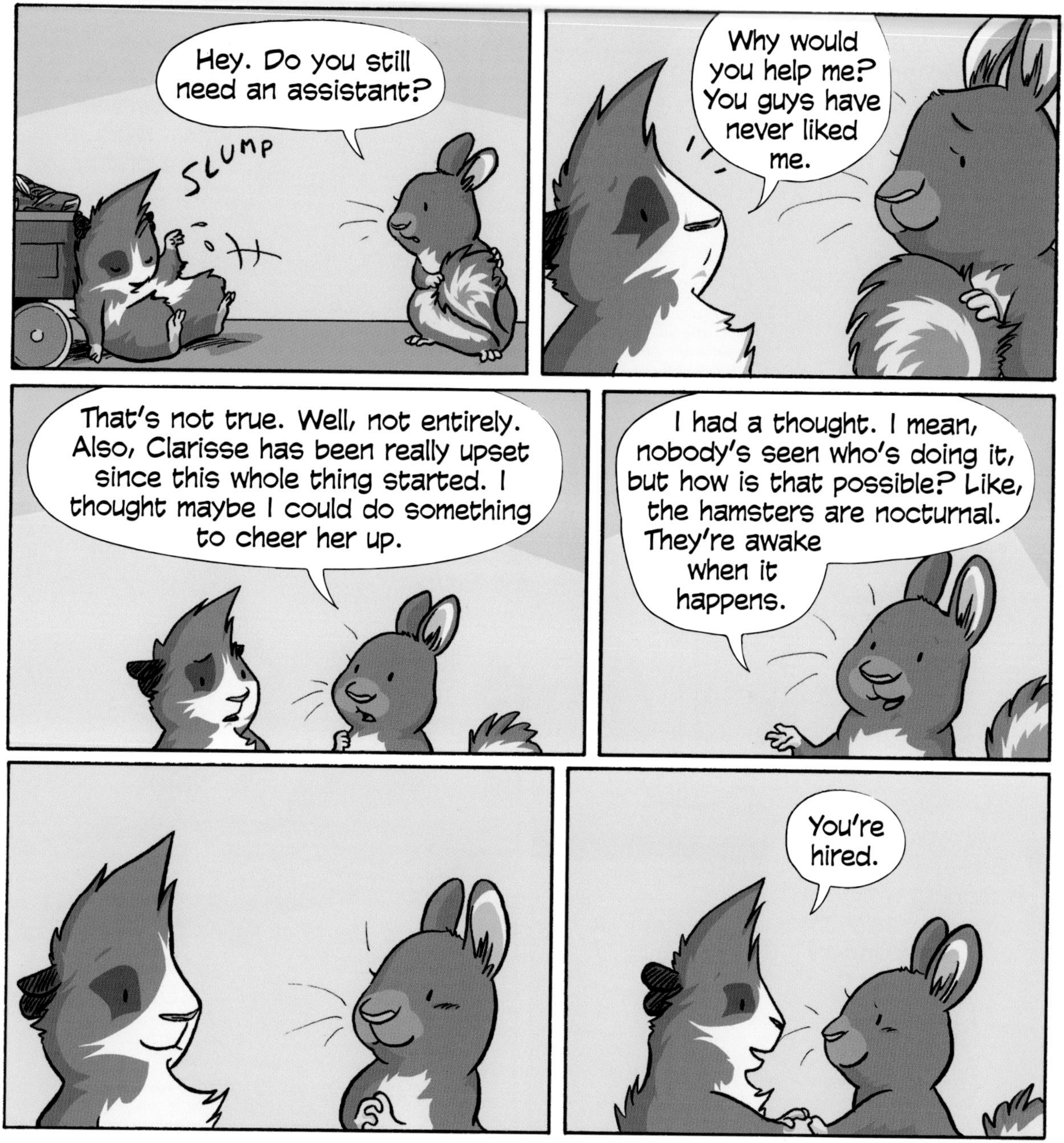
Hey. Do you still need an assistant?
SLUMP
Why would you help me? You guys have never liked me.
That's not true. Well, not entirely. Also, Clarisse has been really upset since this whole thing started. I thought maybe I could do something to cheer her up.
I had a thought. I mean, nobody's seen who's doing it, but how is that possible? Like, the hamsters are nocturnal. They're awake when it happens.
You're hired.

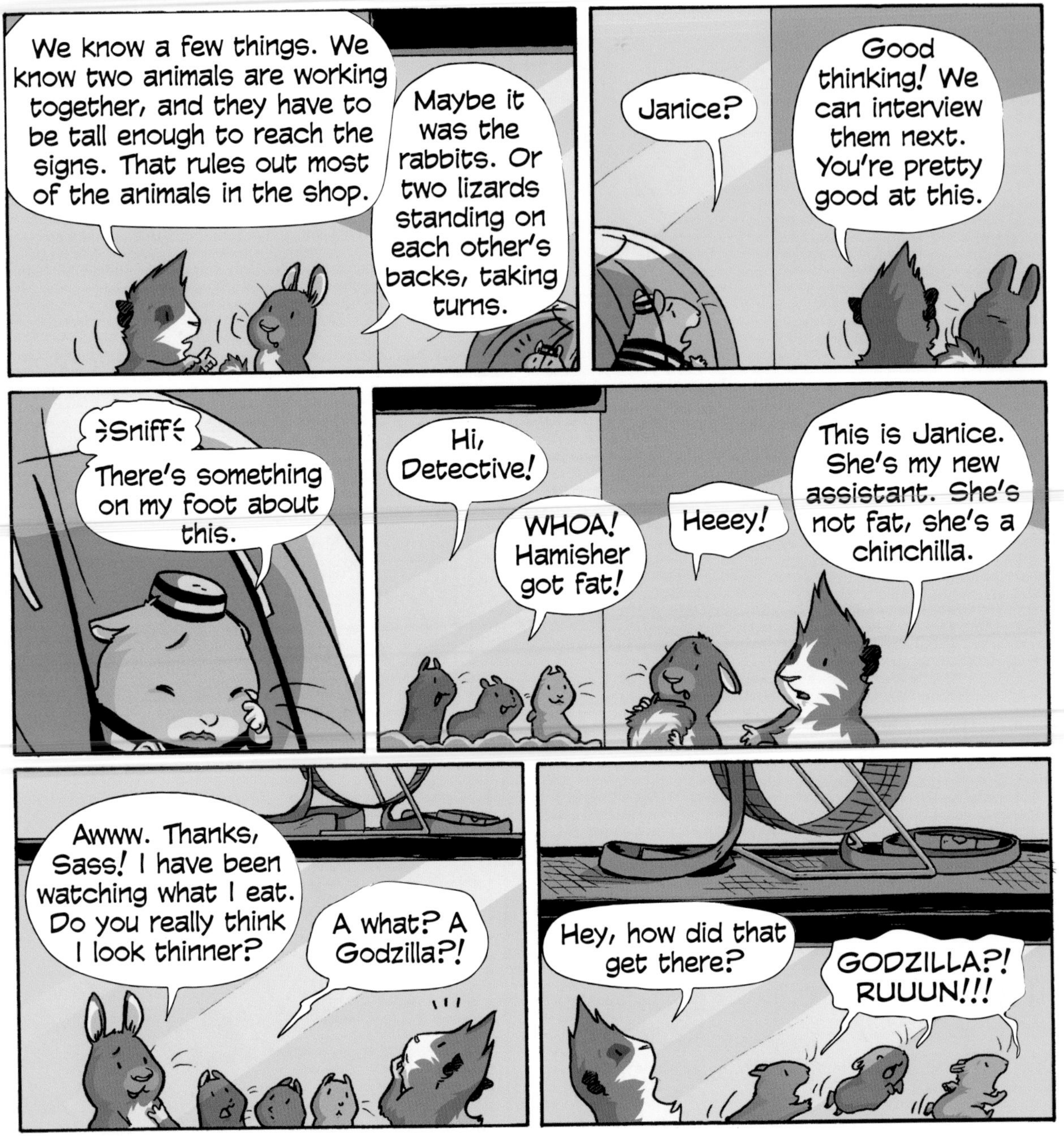
We know a few things. We know two animals are working together, and they have to be tall enough to reach the signs. That rules out most of the animals in the shop.
Maybe it was the rabbits. Or two lizards standing on each other's backs, taking turns.
Janice?
Good thinking! We can interview them next. You're pretty good at this.
⪢Sniff⪡
There's something on my foot about this.
Hi, Detective!
WHOA! Hamisher got fat!
Heeey!
This is Janice. She's my new assistant. She's not fat, she's a chinchilla.
Awww. Thanks, Sass! I have been watching what I eat. Do you really think I look thinner?
A what? A Godzilla?!
Hey, how did that get there?
GODZILLA?! RUUUN!!!

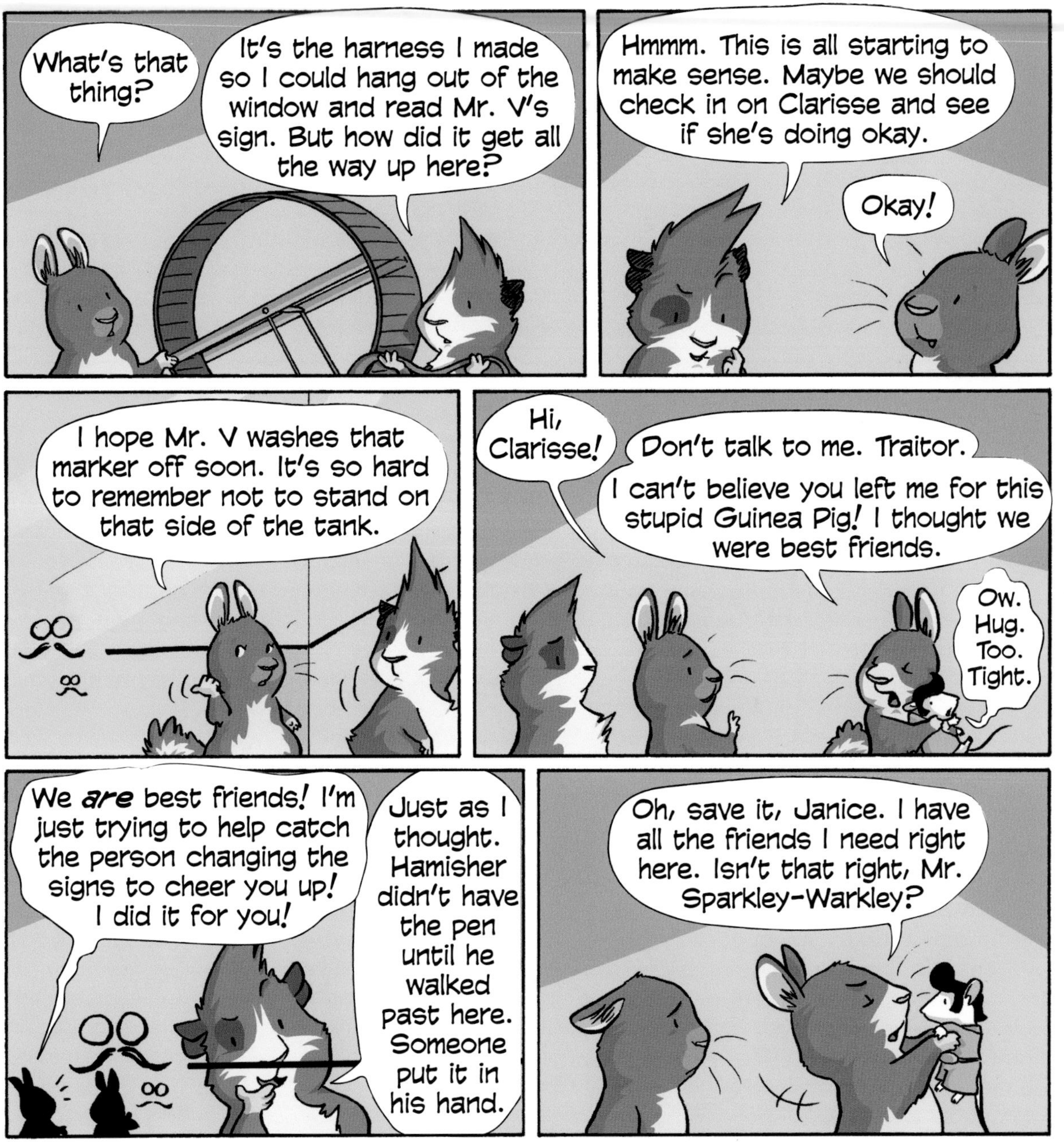
What's that thing?
It's the harness I made so I could hang out of the window and read Mr. V's sign. But how did it get all the way up here?
Hmmm. This is all starting to make sense. Maybe we should check in on Clarisse and see if she's doing okay.
Okay!
I hope Mr. V washes that marker off soon. It's so hard to remember not to stand on that side of the tank.
Hi, Clarisse!
Don't talk to me. Traitor.
I can't believe you left me for this stupid Guinea Pig! I thought we were best friends.
Ow. Hug. Too. Tight.
We *are* best friends! I'm just trying to help catch the person changing the signs to cheer you up! I did it for you!
Just as I thought. Hamisher didn't have the pen until he walked past here. Someone put it in his hand.
Oh, save it, Janice. I have all the friends I need right here. Isn't that right, Mr. Sparkley-Warkley?

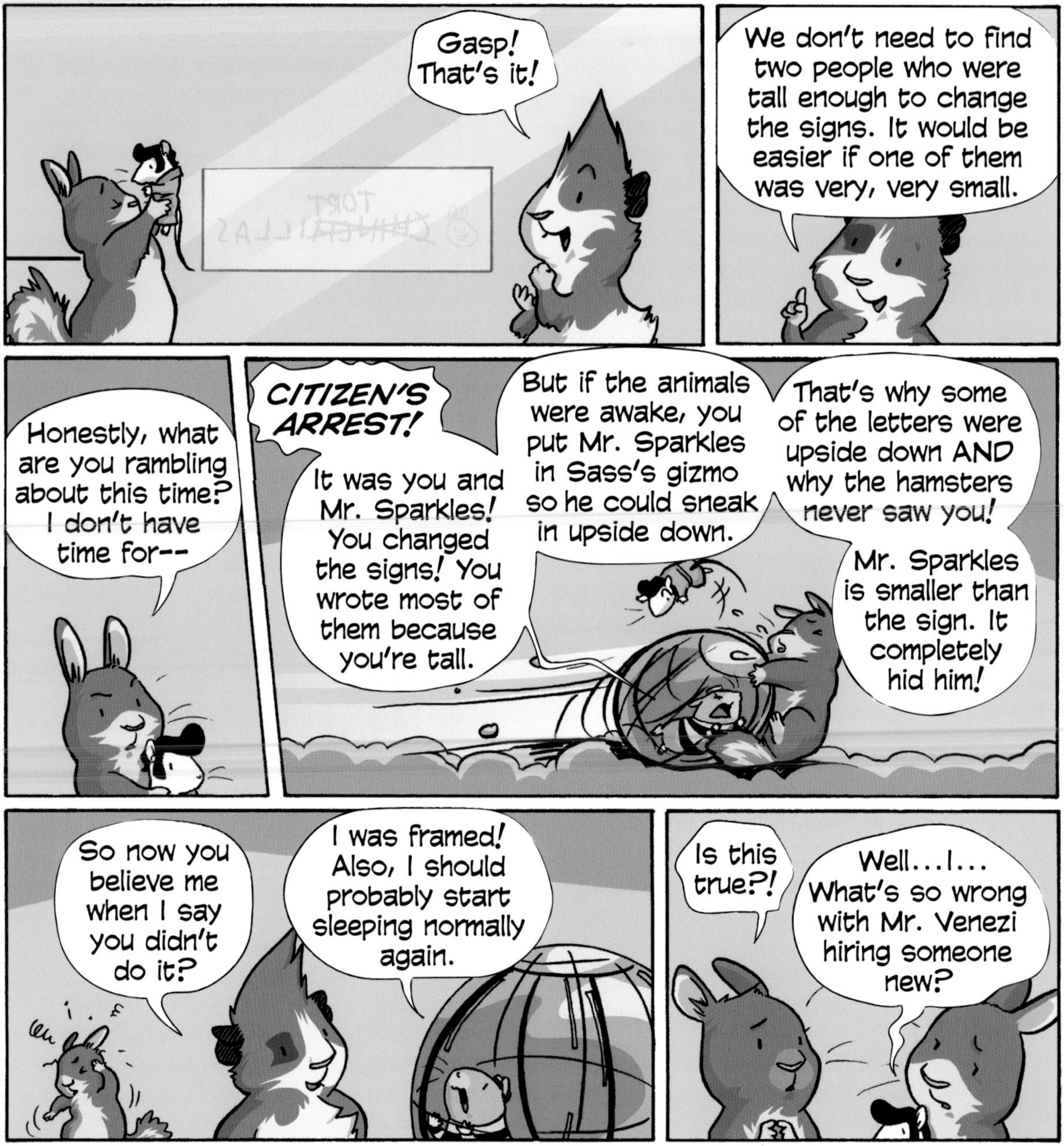
Gasp! That's it!
TORT CHINCHILLAS
We don't need to find two people who were tall enough to change the signs. It would be easier if one of them was very, very small.
Honestly, what are you rambling about this time? I don't have time for--
CITIZEN'S ARREST!
It was you and Mr. Sparkles! You changed the signs! You wrote most of them because you're tall.
But if the animals were awake, you put Mr. Sparkles in Sass's gizmo so he could sneak in upside down.
That's why some of the letters were upside down AND why the hamsters never saw you!
Mr. Sparkles is smaller than the sign. It completely hid him!
So now you believe me when I say you didn't do it?
I was framed! Also, I should probably start sleeping normally again.
Is this true?!
Well...I... What's so wrong with Mr. Venezi hiring someone new?

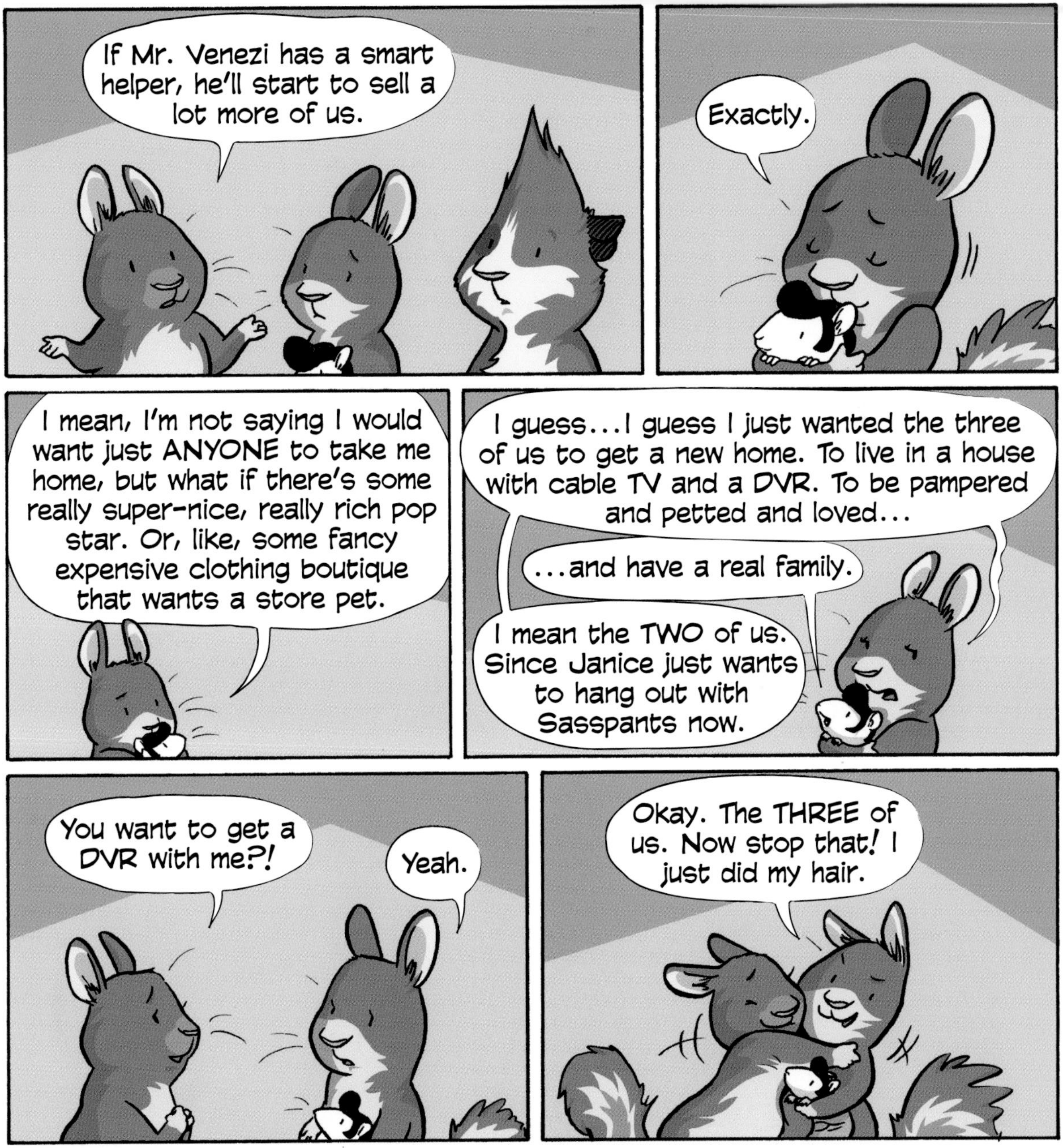
If Mr. Venezi has a smart helper, he'll start to sell a lot more of us.
Exactly.
I mean, I'm not saying I would want just ANYONE to take me home, but what if there's some really super-nice, really rich pop star. Or, like, some fancy expensive clothing boutique that wants a store pet.
I guess... I guess I just wanted the three of us to get a new home. To live in a house with cable TV and a DVR. To be pampered and petted and loved...
...and have a real family.
I mean the TWO of us. Since Janice just wants to hang out with Sasspants now.
You want to get a DVR with me?!
Yeah.
Okay. The THREE of us. Now stop that! I just did my hair.

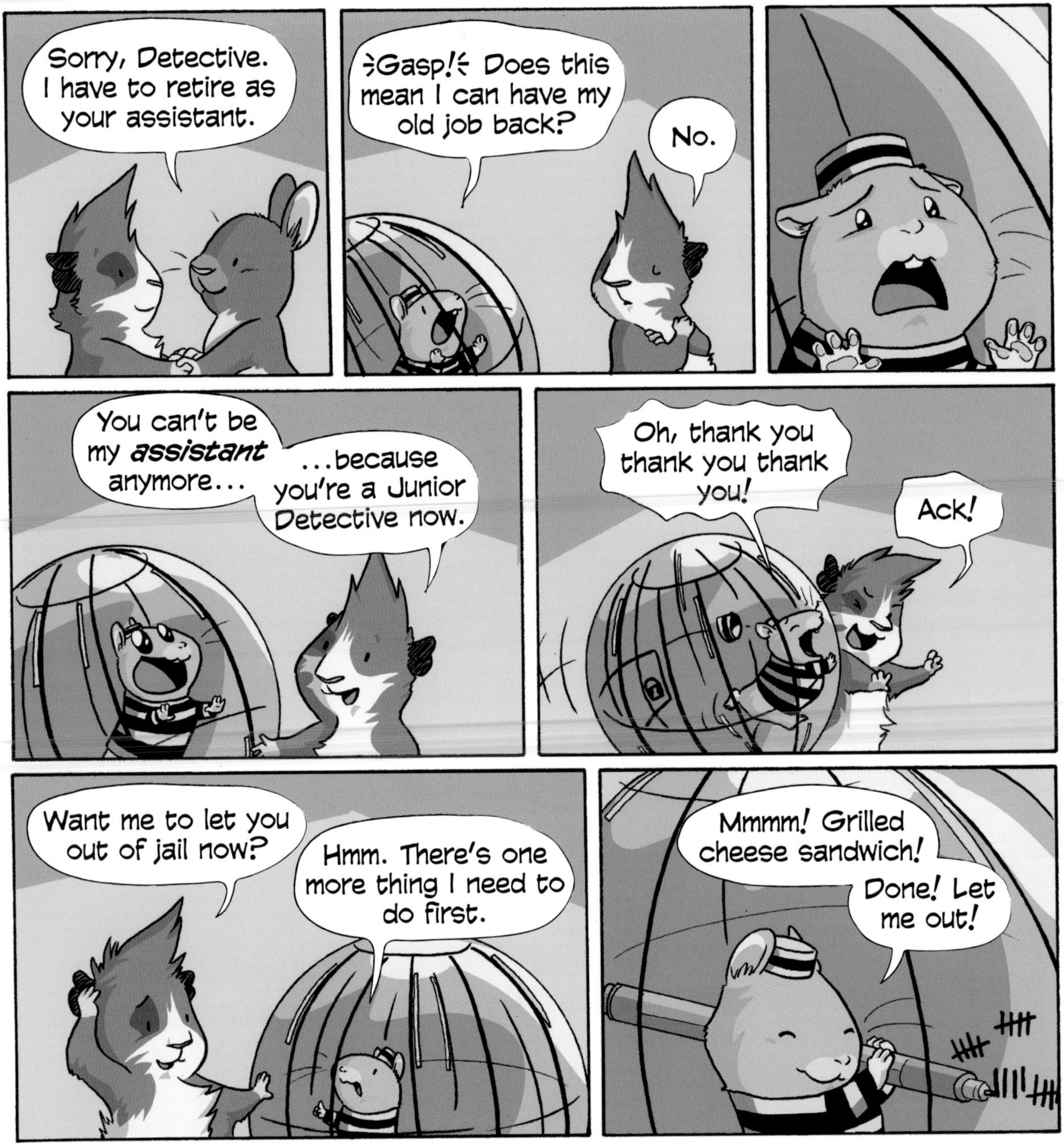
Sorry, Detective. I have to retire as your assistant.
Gasp! Does this mean I can have my old job back?
No.
You can't be my *assistant* anymore...
...because you're a Junior Detective now.
Oh, thank you thank you thank you!
Ack!
Want me to let you out of jail now?
Hmm. There's one more thing I need to do first.
Mmmm! Grilled cheese sandwich!
Done! Let me out!

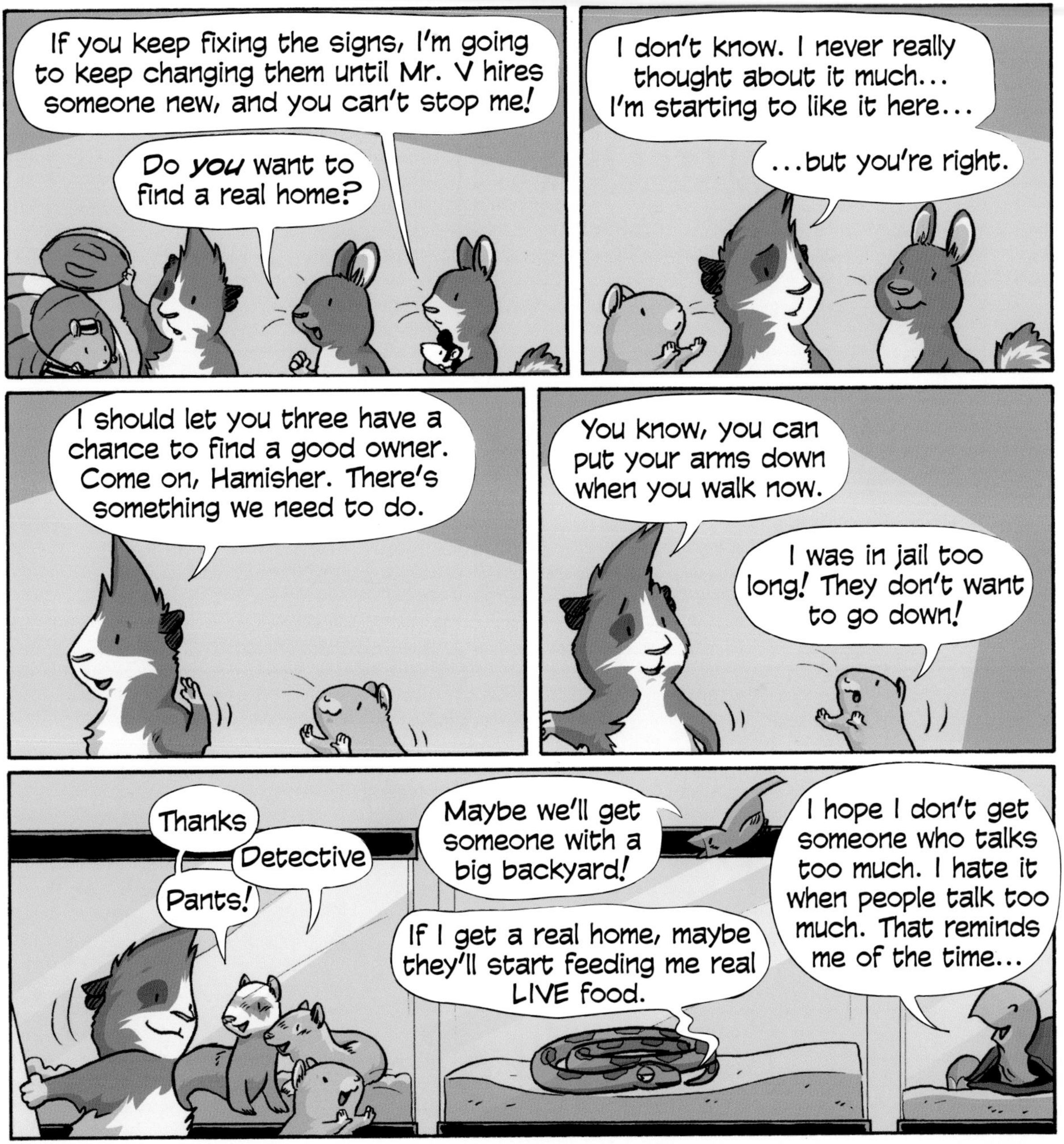
If you keep fixing the signs, I'm going to keep changing them until Mr. V hires someone new, and you can't stop me!
Do *you* want to find a real home?
I don't know. I never really thought about it much... I'm starting to like it here...
...but you're right.
I should let you three have a chance to find a good owner. Come on, Hamisher. There's something we need to do.
You know, you can put your arms down when you walk now.
I was in jail too long! They don't want to go down!
Thanks
Detective
Pants!
Maybe we'll get someone with a big backyard!
If I get a real home, maybe they'll start feeding me real LIVE food.
I hope I don't get someone who talks too much. I hate it when people talk too much. That reminds me of the time...

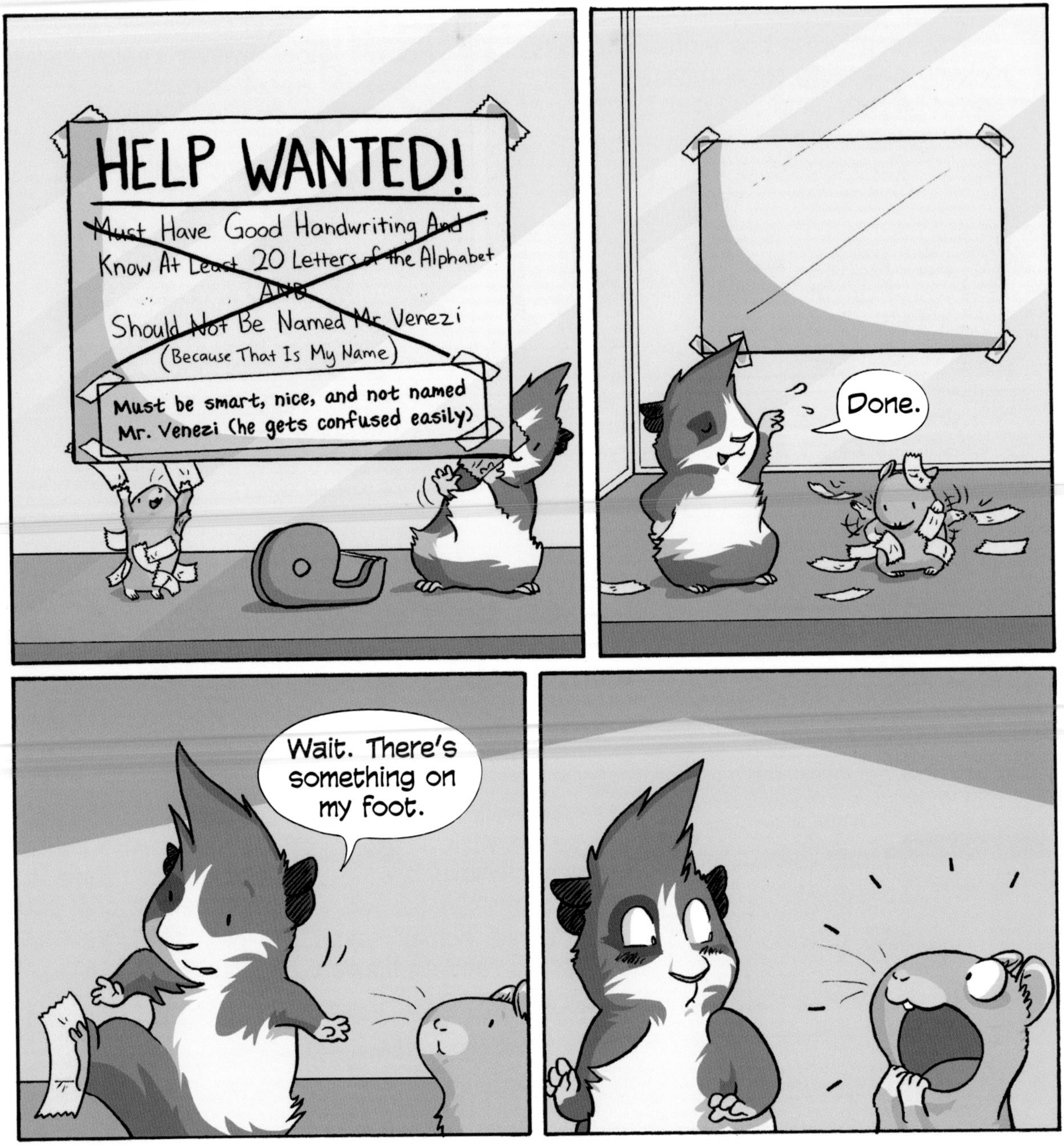
HELP WANTED!
Must Have Good Handwriting And
Know At Least 20 Letters of the Alphabet
AND
Should Not Be Named Mr Venezi
(Because That Is My Name)
Must be smart, nice, and not named Mr. Venezi (he gets confused easily)
Done.
Wait. There's something on my foot.

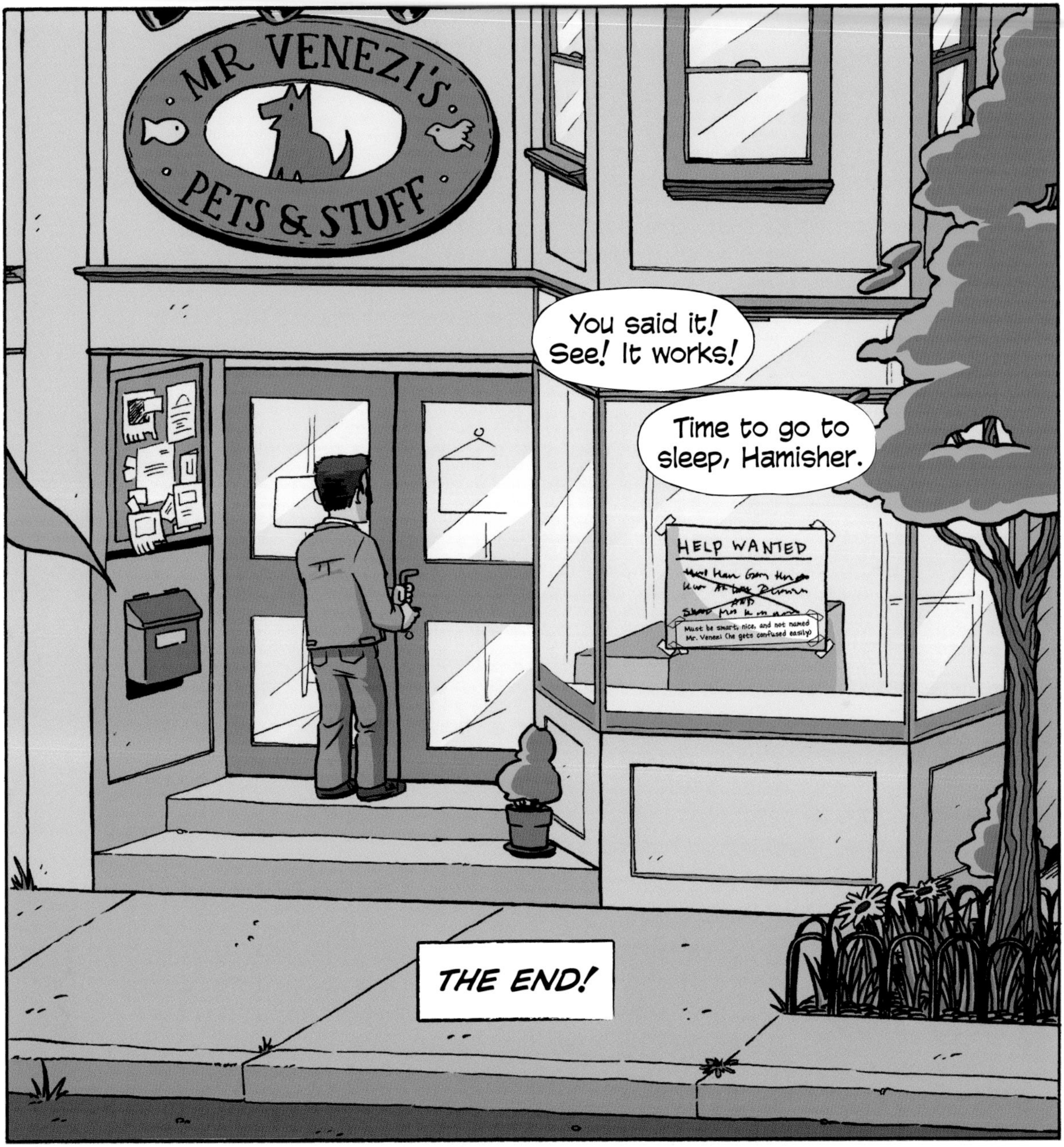
MR. VENEZI'S
PETS & STUFF
You said it! See! It works!
Time to go to sleep, Hamisher.
HELP WANTED
Must be smart, nice, and not named Mr. Venezi (he gets confused easily)
THE END!

HAMISHER EXPLAINS...

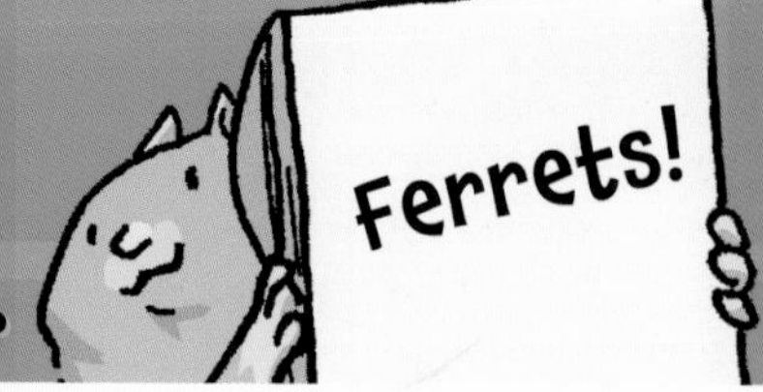
Ferrets!

Sass keeps telling me that ferrets aren't snakes with big beards (or long mustaches). They aren't related to snakes or to hamsters at all. Ferrets are more like weasels, minks, otters, badgers, and skunks. Wild ferrets can even spray a bad smell when they get angry or afraid, which stinks for the person who made them mad!

Wadsworth and Toobusy aren't nocturnal like me, but they sleep A LOT. Night and day! 14 to 20 hours. It's called being ***crepuscular***. That doesn't mean they eat crepes all the time. It means they are only fully awake for a few hours when the sun comes up and for a few hours when the sun goes down—pretty much when Mr. V has just closed or is about to open the shop. When they are awake, they are AWAKE, running around like crazy. When they are asleep, it takes an army to wake them. You can pick them up, and they keep on sleeping. I bet it's because they have really good dreams. Maybe about junior detective dragons.

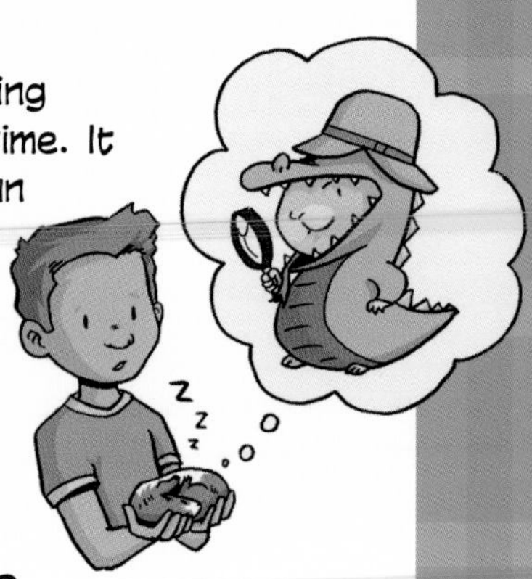

Ferrets have been around FOREVER—or for at least 2,000 years. There are scenes of ferrets walking on leashes painted on the walls of ancient Egyptian tombs! It wasn't until the 1980s that modern people started keeping ferrets as pets. Now ferrets are the third most popular pet in the United States! Right behind hamsters and hamsters!

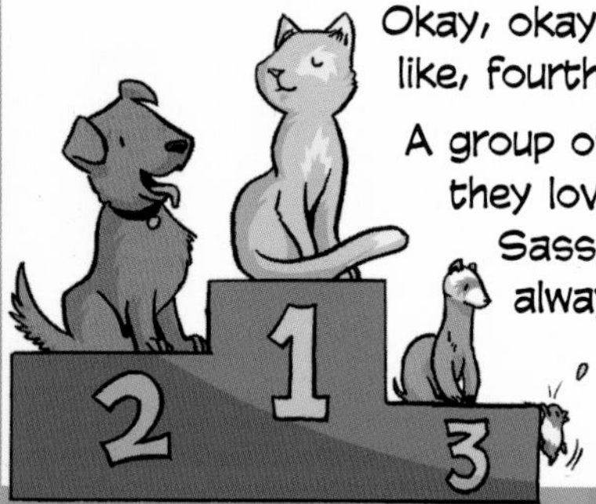
1
2
3

Okay, okay. Behind cats and dogs. But I bet hamsters are, like, fourth.

A group of ferrets is called a business of ferrets, because they love to wear business suits. Are you sure that's right, Sass? Maybe it's because, when they are awake, they always look busy!

Owning ferrets is actually illegal in some places in the United States, such as California and

New York City. That's because ferrets are sneeeaky. They can fit into tiny holes and crawl under doors! Some folk think that makes ferrets dangerous, but a lot of people think that makes them helpful! In the 1880s, they were hired by the president of the United States to creep into holes and chase all the rats out of the White House. Ferrets are also used as electrician's assistants, sneaking under floorboards carrying cables. In London, England, back in the 1980s, ferrets did the wiring for the TV broadcast of Prince Charles and Lady Diana's wedding!

Hmmm. So I guess they actually ***are*** in "business."

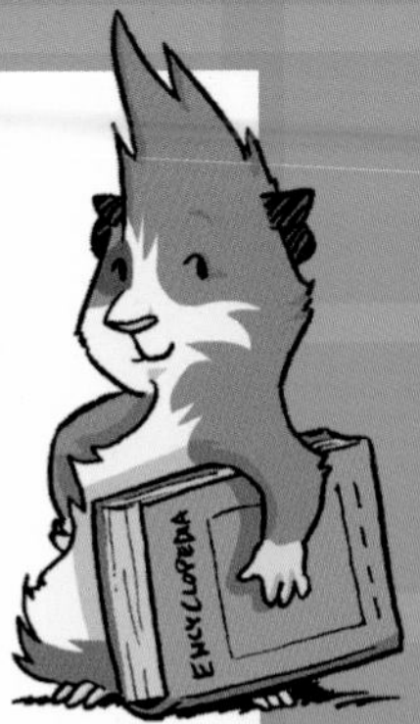
ENCYCLOPEDIA

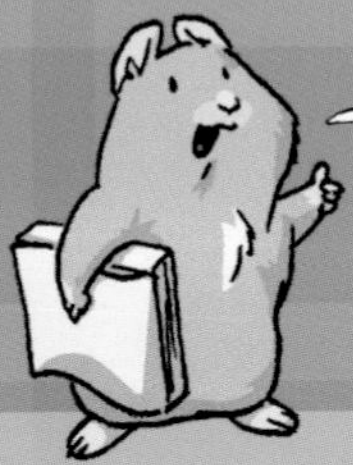

Now that I'm a Junior Detective I should talk like one! Here are some mysterious terms!

SLEUTH is another name for someone who solves crimes. But if you call Sass a sleuth, you're calling her a dog! The sleuthhound was a kind of bloodhound that smelled great! Well...it had a really powerful nose. They don't always smell great in the other way.

Speaking of smelly things, a RED HERRING is a type of fish, but it's also a mystery term! If a criminal does something to distract you from the ***real*** crime, that's called a red herring. Like when you say, "Hey, is that an elephant over there?" and then switch your empty ice-cream bowl with your friend's because she still has a scoop of vanilla. The elephant is the fish! (Um...I think I've been hanging out with Mr. Venezi too much.)

In the old days, crooks would drop stinky red herrings on the ground to confuse the bloodhounds. That's a smart trick, but that means criminals had to walk around with fish in their pockets. Ewww.

For more mysterious terms, turn the page!

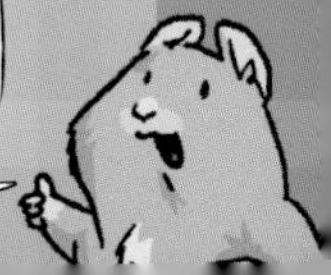

More Mysterious Terms!

Oooh, here's another animal mix-up! The ferrets in this story were goats! Scapegoats, that is. A SCAPEGOAT is the person who gets blamed (or FRAMED) for something they didn't do!

If you are a detective who likes to talk fancy talk, you can say someone purloined something. PURLOIN means the same thing as "steal."

GUMSHOE: A Private Eye. Sass says I'm not allowed to make a joke about this word. But there's something on my...you know the rest.

ALIBI: Proof that you were somewhere else when a crime took place.

HUNCH: Rhymes with lunch! Also brunch! And flunch! This is when you have an idea about what happened, but you don't have the facts to back it up yet.

CLUE: This comes from an older word, "clew," which means "a ball of yarn." Follow the yarn and you'll find, well, the rest of the yarn.

DEDUCE: When you deduce something, it's the opposite of a hunch. This is when you have enough clues to make a guess.

DRAGONS: Love grilled cheese sandwiches and flying!

DENOUEMENT (day-noo-MONT): This is the end! The solution to the mystery, when everything makes sense!